P9-ARM-775

ABOUT THE BOOK

Washington Irving is well known for his delightful stories of Sleepy Hollow. Less well known is the fact that Irving's success with these stories proved a turning point in the long, bitter controversy between the fledgling United States and England, which as a nation prided itself on literary accomplishment. English critics proclaimed that no American would ever write anything worthwhile, and indeed, before Irving, most American writings were slavish imitations of English masters.

In this three-part source book George Sanderlin presents us with a brief but comprehensive biography of Irving, excerpts from his works, and an insight into this fascinating debate over America's ability to produce a writer. Said one critic: "No man in the republic of letters has been more overrated than Mr. Washington Irving." Said another: "Washington Irving's style is undoubtedly one of the most finished and agreeable forms in which the English language has ever been presented."

George Sanderlin has compiled a valuable collection of writings, about Irving, his times, and his legacy of characters. This is a challenging and informative book that will stimulate readers to form their own opinions of one of America's legendary storytellers.

Washington Irving: As Others Saw Him

by George Sanderlin

Coward, McCann & Geoghegan, Inc.
New York

The author gratefully acknowledges permission to reprint the following:

From *Classic Americans: A Study of Eminent American Writers from Irving to Whitman,* by Henry Seidel Canby. Copyright 1959 by Henry Seidel Canby and reprinted with the permission of Russell & Russell.

From *A Many-Windowed House: Collected Essays on American Writers And American Writing,* by Malcolm Cowley, edited, with an Introduction by Henry Dan Piper. Copyright 1970 by Southern Illinois University Press. Reprinted by permission of Southern Illinois University Press.

From *The Literary Situation,* by Malcolm Cowley. Copyright 1947 by The Viking Press, Inc., and reprinted with their permission.

From *Essays on American Literature in Honor of Jay B. Hubbell,* edited by Clarence Gohdes. Copyright 1967 by the Duke University Press and reprinted with their permission.

From *Washington Irving, Esquire,* by George S. Hellman, Copyright 1925 by Random House and reprinted with their permission.

From *Expression in America,* by Ludwig Lewisohn. Copyright 1932 by Ludwig Lewisohn. Reprinted by permission of Mrs. Ludwig Lewisohn.

Contents

Washington Irving at age 26,
oil painting by John Wesley Jarvis.

The Life of
WASHINGTON IRVING

"WHO READS AN AMERICAN BOOK"

"In the four quarters of the globe, who reads an American book?" asked a scornful British critic.

The year was 1820. Settlers were streaming across the Mississippi. Canals were being dug. Axes rang in the woods. Smoke-belching steamboats appeared on the Hudson, and within a few years an "iron horse" would startle the cows grazing beside the first railroad tracks in Pennsylvania. Yet swamp grass grew in Pennsylvania Avenue in front of the White House, the Creek Indians stirred restlessly in Alabama, and much of the land was still one vast forest.

"Forced to live by the sweat of their brow—the farmer, the husbandman, and the woodsman, had little time, and less inclination, for literary pursuits," declared another English observer.

When Americans adopted Jefferson's Declaration of Independence, the world had paid attention. Politics and the "rights of man" were thought to be understood in the New World Republic. But "polite literature"—poetry, the drama, the short story and essay? No. The arts belonged to the Old World, to Europe with its kings and bishops, its cathedrals, its culture.

One American changed all that. In this very year, 1820,

Washington Irving published his *Sketch Book*. In it, Ichabod Crane, tugging his sleeves down toward his bony wrists, courted the fair Katrina and fled in terror from the headless horseman of Sleepy Hollow. In it Rip Van Winkle rubbed his eyes as he awoke on a "green knoll"—and with him awoke American literature.

"From the moment that the writings of Mr. Irving became popular, it has been the fashion to admire and extol American literature," an Englishman admitted. "One of the finest things ever written," the poet Byron said of an essay in *The Sketch Book,* and he claimed to know the book "by heart."

From that crucial first success to the present, through Melville's *Moby Dick* to Hemingway's *The Old Man and the Sea,* world interest in American literature has never ceased.

Washington Irving has been accused of being an idler. He frittered away and abandoned his law studies while he toured Europe or enjoyed the plays and dances of Manhattan with his exuberant young friends. But his success was something more than an accident. It was the result of a powerful ambition for literary fame and a discipline that kept him writing through illness, bankruptcy, and the tragic death of the girl he loved.

As America's first professional author, Irving devoted years to the mastery of his craft. He wrote hundreds of thousands of words, in journals which covered almost every day of his life up to late middle age. Thus, he developed a readable and entertaining style.

He portrayed memorable characters from history, and, indeed, created legends for a land that was still raw and new. He was a pioneer in the development of the short story and a master of the informal essay. His humor, his reasonableness, his old-fashioned eighteenth-century courtesy made a winning combination.

There were other Americans writing in the early 1800's —pamphleteers, satirists (the "Hartford Wits"), novelists, playwrights, poets including authors of "epics." But there was only one American who reversed the judgment of the Old World that Americans could not write, only one American, at first, who achieved international fame. That was Washington Irving, who became, like Chaucer, the "morning star" of a new literature, the imaginative writings of the American Republic.

A BOY OF MANHATTAN

Washington Irving came into the world on April 3, 1783, in a town of 20,000—New York—still blackened by wartime fires and occupied by British redcoats. He was the eleventh child of a Presbyterian merchant, William Irving, and his tenderhearted wife, Sarah.

"[George] Washington's work is ended, and the child shall be named after him," declared Sarah Irving, who had nursed American prisoners during the war.

Although the family was not wealthy, Washington, the "baby," was somewhat spoiled by his brothers and sisters. He was sensitive, lovable, a dreamer. Sisters Ann, Catherine, and Sarah liked to play on his feelings by singing sad Highland songs to him. His practical brothers William, Ebenezer, and John were often a wall between him and the harsh world. Another brother, the vagabond Peter, would later share his literary interests.

Washington grew up at 128 William Street, on lower Manhattan. Like most old houses in the eastern United States, this residence had a narrow front, 25 feet wide. But the lot was 156 feet deep, so there was space behind the house for a small garden, full of the scent of flowers and fruit trees.

Here is where his sisters sang their ballads to Washington and told him stories. Here he dreamed of adventures he would have when he grew up.

"When I was very young," said Washington Irving, "every thing was fairy land to me."

He was a happy child, devoted to his pretty mother (of "elegant shape") who had married her Scottish seaman, William Irving, and come to America with him. But Washington did not care for Deacon Irving's Bible reading and daily prayers.

"When I was young," Washington also complained, "I was led to think that somehow or other every thing that was pleasant was wicked!"

Starting at age six, Washington Irving attended a small school in Partition Street, taught by a gimlet-eyed ex-soldier, Benjamin Romaine. A fellow student described Washington as "sluggish and inapt," perhaps because Washington was often staring out a window, listening to the song of a bobolink rather than to Romaine droning on about Latin declensions.

From Romaine Washington did not learn much more than how to read and write, but that was enough. For he found himself transported to the magical world of books.

Sinbad the Sailor, Robinson Crusoe, the characters of Shakespeare—Washington read their stories wide-eyed. The puzzled deacon, seeing Washington poring over his books, dubbed him "the Philosopher." When Washington came upon books about Columbus' discovery of America and the Spanish conquests of Mexico and Peru, he thought he had never read fairy tales so wonderful.

"A book of travel was like a coach at the door," he said. "I must jump in and take a ride!"

He now wrote compositions for his fellow students, changing his style to fit their personalities. In return, they did his arithmetic problems for him.

At fourteen, he decided to run away to sea. He had

wandered along the pierheads jutting out into the East River like tentacles. He had heard the sailors' cries as sails were run up and the great three-masters headed out of the harbor toward Spain. He had sailed his own small boat in the spray of Hell's Gate.

To train for his days in the forecastle, he ate salt pork (which he hated) and slept on the plank floor of his bedroom every night!

But New York was too much fun to leave. A young artist who was courting Washington's sister Catherine showed Washington his sketch book and played the violin for him. And then Washington discovered the nearby John Street Theater, the first home of the drama in New York.

This was a plain red building, set back from the street, with a tunnellike entrance. But inside was another world: two blazing chandeliers, footlights with their tin shades gleaming, boxes, the pit seats, balconies, and a glorious green curtain. "They lifted up a great green cloth," said one backcountry spectator, "and let us look right into the next neighbor's house!"

Washington would attend an early performance here, then hurry home to chime in at family prayers and meekly retire to his bedroom. He would then squeeze out his window, scramble across the woodshed roof and return to the theater in time for the second piece. He wrote a play himself, which has not survived.

He also went squirrel hunting. One day he wandered several miles up the Hudson to an ancient village of quaint yellow brick houses with steep roofs and gables, like an illustration from *Hansel and Gretel*—a village called Sleepy Hollow. He leaned on his rifle and imagined the old Dutch colonists, in their breeches and wide-skirted coats, solemnly deliberating on the neatly trimmed green.

He had a little more schooling under pompous, red-faced Josiah Henderson, an authority on the drama, and

15

under one Jonathan Fiske, a Latinist. Then it was time to follow his brothers to Columbia College or to go to work.

Like many seventeen-year-olds, Washington did not particularly want to do either. He had not chosen a career. He was dreaming, instead, of a shelfful of books written by one Washington Irving. Books about the Spanish conquistadors, about Shakespeare's England, about the pipe-puffing Dutch settlers. . . .

But this, of course, was only a dream. In the Republic of 1799 no one, excluding a few journalists, supported himself by the pen. Farming, law, politics, business—there was a man's work to be done. Benjamin Franklin had been printer, businessman, diplomat. The poet Philip Freneau was a trader, government official, farmer. The novelist Charles Brockden Brown was just going into journalism to make his living. Versifiers Timothy Dwight and Joel Barlow were, respectively, college president and lawyer. What mere American author could compete with the world-renowned works of Byron and Scott, which were not covered by copyright and so were available free to any publisher?

Deacon Irving had hoped for a clergyman among his five sons, but after four disappointments probably expected little of the family dreamer. Reluctantly, Washington opted for the law. He "would overwhelm the guilty—uphold the innocent!" Also, he would thus avoid "the harassing cares of commerce" that his brothers William and Ebenezer encountered in the family business.

What kind of lawyer would Washington Irving have made? The world will never know. Although he studied in several law offices and finally managed to pass his bar examination, he said that a popular story about another law student applied to him.

"I think," the bar examiner said of this student, "that he knows a little law."

"Make it stronger," said a colleague. *"Damned* little!"

16

In 1802, Washington went to read law under Judge Josiah Hoffman, New York's capable attorney general. Hoffman made Washington feel at home among his large family, which included two charming daughters. Washington flirted with the brilliant teen-ager Ann, but it was the younger Matilda—pale, dark-haired, shy—whom he felt strangely drawn to. Soon he was giving her drawing lessons.

His brother Peter often came to the law office to chat about literature and the drama. And Washington had lost none of his enthusiasm for these subjects. He now began to keep a journal, to practice his writing. Sailing up the Hudson, carrying the flute he had learned to play, he had earlier described the Catskill Mountains:

"I lay on the deck and watched them [the Catskills] . . . sometimes seeming to approach; at other times to recede; now almost melting into hazy distance, now burnished by the setting sun, until, in the evening, they printed themselves against the glowing sky in the deep purple of an Italian landscape."

When Peter became editor of the *Morning Chronicle,* Washington burst into print. In that paper, in November, 1802, appeared the first essay by *"Jonathan Oldstyle, Gent."* Jonathan Oldstyle was Washington Irving, who now wrote nine pieces about the follies of New Yorkers, especially as displayed in the theater.

"In one of the scenes," he commented on one play, "I was diverted with the stupidity of a corporal and his men, who sung a dull song, and talked a great deal about nothing. . . . What this scene had to do with the rest of the piece, I could not comprehend; I suspect it was a part of some other play, thrust in here by accident."

Washington's writing was rather amateurish, but spirited. Soon he was recognized in select circles as "a gentleman of . . . literary acquirements."

In 1803, he accompanied Judge Hoffman on a business trip through the wilderness to Montreal. It was a rugged journey, made by jolting oxcart under leaden skies. "We . . . dragged along—wet to the skin wading through mud holes—it seemed as if the whole forest was under water," Washington wrote in a journal he kept of the trip.

He survived, but on his return he seemed "peaked." His brothers, who long ago had concluded that Washington was not only talented but of delicate health, were worried. They decided now that a grand tour of Europe would improve his condition. They would pay his expenses, and Judge Hoffman agreed to give him leave from the law office.

When they told Washington, he thought his boyhood dreams had come true. London, Rome, Florence, Paris— he would see the famous places he had read about. He was so excited about going that he was surprised to feel a stab of regret when he looked into Matilda's eyes and said good-bye.

"I will send you drawings from Italy," he promised.

On May 19, 1804, he embarked, but he had to be helped up the side of the ship.

"There's a chap who will go overboard before we get across," prophesied the captain.

Then the ship slid away from its anchorage. The faces of his brothers blurred, and Washington felt himself alone, and suddenly homesick, on "the vast space of waters that separates the hemispheres . . . like a blank page in existence."

TOURING EUROPE

Washington soon recovered from his homesickness, and his corpse did not "go overboard" as the captain had prophesied.

"The sea has much degenerated since ancient days," he wrote a friend. "Then one could hardly sail out of sight of land without meeting Neptune and his suite in full gallop, whereas I have passed across the wide Atlantic without seeing even a mermaid!"

These high spirits were to last. Washington toured Europe like a small boy let out of school. Dances, plays, pretty girls—yes; archaeology, close study of languages—no. But he did keep the most detailed journal yet, with descriptions of people, scenes, customs. He was learning to write.

"The land rose from the shore into vast mountains of rock that lifted their snowy heads far above the clouds." Thus he described their first landfall, Cape Penas, Spain.

The women of Bordeaux made the following impression: "How often in walking the street, do I see a fair nymph before me. . . . I hurry after her . . . she turns her face towards me—the charm is broken. . . . I see a wide mouth, small black eyes, cheeks highly rouged and hair greased with ancient oil and twisted from the forehead to the chin till it resembles the head dress of a Medusa!"

From Bordeaux, Washington traveled toward Italy with a boisterous Dr. Henry of Lancaster, Pennsylvania. The little doctor clowned and flirted while Washington sat quietly in their coach.

"You are always thinking," a young French traveler told Washington, "but you never say anything!"

Washington was more talkative in the friendly English and American colony at Genoa. Clad in "gray frock, white waistcoat, frilled shirt, black silk breeches, and silk stockings" he went lightheartedly to balls, where he noted:

"The innocent familiarities that prevail between young people of both sexes in America and England is unknown in this country and to press the *ruby lips* of a fair damsel would be a howling abomination. . . . To kiss the *hand* of a married woman, however, is a fashionable . . . mode of salutation."

He remained in Genoa for two months, learning a little Italian but devoting more time to the theater. He developed a romantic interest in banditti; in his journal he described the execution of one Joseph Musso, an Italian Robin Hood:

"He appeared to be about five feet eight inches, stout and well set, of a dark complexion with strong but good features and immense eyebrows. . . . He was shot on the banks of a small river . . . and suffered his sentence in a very manly decent manner."

Then he left on an American ship for Sicily. En route a strange sail came over the horizon. Soon a band of men with daggers in their sashes—men "of a dark complexion" with "immense eyebrows"—swarmed aboard the American ship. This time the banditti had come to Washington Irving!

They seized all the brandy and quicksilver aboard. One of them thumbed through Washington's letters of introduction to individuals throughout Europe, but threw them down in disgust.

"This is a fellow who runs all around the world!" he said.

The pirates sailed off without injuring anyone, but for some time afterward Washington, who had behaved bravely, had nightmares about the buccaneers.

At Messina, in Sicily, he saw a line of ships enter the strait between Sicily and Italy. White sails, black hulls with yellow bands running lengthwise—like the marking of a bumblebee—and yawning gunports spaced along the yellow bands, to sting.

"It was . . . the English fleet," wrote Irving. "In a short time Lord Nelson's ship the *Victory* hove in sight—they all advanced most majestically up the Straits. . . . It was very pleasing to observe with what promptness and dexterity the signals were made, answered and obeyed. The fleet seemed as a body of men under perfect discipline."

While in Sicily, Irving "mounted Vesuvius at night, when we had a tremendous view of the crater, a stream of red-hot lava, etc. We approached near enough to the latter to thrust our sticks into it."

In Rome, Irving made a friend of the young American painter Washington Allston, who praised his drawings. Irving was awed by Allston's "elevated and poetic mind. . . . His eyes would dilate; his pale countenance would flush; he would breathe quick . . . when excited by any object of grandeur and sublimity."

"Why might I not remain here, and turn painter?" Irving asked himself enviously.

But Washington Irving always understood his own limitations. He was *not* a painter. He departed for Paris—"leaving Florence on your left and Venice on your right [unseen]," grumbled his brother William, who wished Washington to seek out the centers of culture.

In Paris there were more parties and plays to attend, more "frail nymphs that wander about" to be observed in the gardens. Then on to "famous and foggy" London, and more theater-going. One performance was interrupted by an actor's dramatic announcement: Nelson had just won a decisive victory at Trafalgar, but had fallen on deck, mortally wounded. Napolean's hopes of invading England were vanquished. Irving made his way that night through tumultuous, cheering throngs.

He sailed for New York in January, 1806. He had dutifully visited a number of art galleries and ruins, but he had not really done justice to European culture. He had, however, measurably improved his writing. His journal was now less formal, less dull, more concise, and vivid, as in this scene from the homeward voyage:

"Don Pedro flaunting about in a great coat and wet underclothes—too lazy to change them. Clark reading a book of children's fables. Eliza reading. Naval manners— Miss Bayley holding her work in one Hand, the other arm on Admiral's shoulder, who is seated on my trunk in his dirty robe de chambre reading."

He landed during a snowstorm on March 24, 1806. Suddenly, he could scarcely wait to see his brothers and sisters, Judge Hoffman's affectionate family, vivacious Ann —and Matilda.

"I recollect my meeting with Matilda as if it was yesterday," wrote Washington Irving. "She entered full of eagerness, yet shy from natural timidity . . . and from the idea of my being a *travelled man,* instead of a stripling student —However what a difference the interval had made. . . . There was a softness and delicacy in her form and look, a countenance of that eloquent expression, yet that mantling modesty—I thought I had never beheld any thing so lovely."

A TRAGIC LOVE

In November, 1806, Irving passed his bar examination. According to legend, he then acquired one client—whom he abandoned!

He spent more time meeting with a lively group of young men, "The Lads of Kilkenny," in a kind of clubhouse on the Passaic River. All were interested in writing; several of them, under Washington's leadership, got out a series of anonymous yellow-backed pamphlets, about the size of a TV guide: *Salmagundi; or, The Whim-Whams and Opinions of Launcelot Langstaff, & Others.* The first was published in January, 1807.

The appearance of these pamphlets over the next thirteen months, containing a total of sixty-five essays, created a sensation. For the anonymous authors high-handedly announced that they would "instruct the young, reform the old, correct the town, and castigate the age." Readers might find "their likenesses" and "those of their neighbors" in these mocking essays.

(A "salmagundi" was a hash containing herring, oil, vinegar, pepper, and onions. The makers of this literary hash—Washington, his brother William, James Paulding, and a typographer David Longworth—met secretly, like bank robbers, in Longworth's bookstore to prepare their copy.)

Everyone hastened to read the latest issue of *Salmagundi* to see whose "likeness" he could discover therein. Who was the flirt "Sophie Sparkle" supposed to be? Who was the politician "Dabble"? The dilettante "Ding-Dong"?

"We begin to suspect that many people read our numbers merely for their amusement, without paying any attention to the serious truths conveyed in every page," protested Washington Irving, tongue in cheek. He wrote most of the essays, in the tradition of English eighteenth-century satire but with an added American zest. They laughed at New York society and national politics and contained some good dramatic criticism.

When the authors became known, Irving's reputation was enhanced. He and his brother Peter then had the idea of writing a comic history of New York. Washington Irving started this work in 1808, but soon another concern began to preoccupy him.

Deacon Irving had died in October, 1807. The years were passing. Did he wish to live all his life as a carefree bachelor?

He and Matilda now "saw each other every day," he wrote, "and I became excessively attached to her. Her shyness wore off by degrees. The more I saw of her the more reason I had to admire her."

Ann had said that people began by admiring *her* but "ended by loving Matilda." So it was with Washington Irving. But what were his prospects?

"I had gone on blindly, like a boy in Love, but now I began to open my eyes and be miserable," he wrote. "I had nothing in purse nor in expectation. . . . I became low spirited and disheartened and did not know what was to become of me."

Into this turmoil stepped an understanding Judge Hoffman, with a suggestion.

"He urged me to return to my studies," wrote Washington. "And that in case I could make myself capable of undertaking legal concerns he would take me into partnership with him and give me his daughter. Nothing could be more generous!"

Washington's spirits soared. Fate, in the person of Josiah Hoffman, had settled his future. He plunged back into the horrid law studies, determined to become a pillar of the community. The dream of a shelfful of books written by Washington Irving was set aside. Matilda was more important.

But one day Matilda "was taken ill with a cold. . . . She grew rapidly worse, and fell into a consumption. . . . Her malady was rapid in its career. . . . For three days and nights I did not leave the house and scarcely slept.

"I was by her when she died—all the family was assembled round her, some praying others weeping, for she was adored by them all. I was the last one she looked upon—

"I have told you as briefly as I could what if I were to tell with all the incidents and feelings that accompanied it would fill volumes. She was but seventeen years old when she died."

Thus Washington Irving wrote, years later, in a manuscript fragment never published. Matilda died April 26, 1809.

The course of his life was irrevocably changed. It was not his destiny to be the pillar of any community or a conventional professional man. He abandoned the law. He was never to marry. It would take ten years of miscellaneous activity before he really found himself again.

"The romance of life," he said, "is past."

WAR AND BANKRUPTCY

While falling in love with Matilda, Washington had completed work on the *History of New York*. Now he "seemed to care for nothing—the world was a blank to me"—yet he had a manuscript ready to be published.

To advertise it, he thought of a clever "hoax." He placed a "missing persons" notice in the New York *Evening Post,* asking anyone seeing "a small elderly gentleman, dressed in an old black coat and cocked hat" to inform the paper. This gentleman, "Diedrich Knickerbocker," was feared to be "not entirely in his right mind."

Eleven days later "A TRAVELLER" reported seeing Knickerbocker on the road to Albany, "much fatigued." Ten days after that Knickerbocker's New York "Landlord" wrote in that the old gentleman had left a *"very curious kind of a written book"* which the Landlord would have to "dispose of" to cover Knickerbocker's unpaid bill.

And then, at last, in December, 1809, appeared "Diedrich Knickerbocker's" *History of New York.*

It was a huge, Sunday-sized chronicle of the past of New Amsterdam (New York under the Dutch). The "renowned Wouter Van Twiller, who erect . . . had not a little the appearance of a beer barrel on skids," presided over the early Councils. Later "William the Testy . . . a brisk, wiry, waspish little old gentleman" banned smoking—which led to the "Pipe Plot" and a "fatal schism" or division into two political parties, the *"Long Pipes"* and the *"Short Pipes."*

William the Testy was, like Thomas Jefferson, a mechanical genius (he invented "carts that went before the horses") and, also like Jefferson, a vivisectionist (he lived on an estate called "Dog's Misery"). Finally, "sturdy, rawboned" Peter Stuyvesant strode forth on his wooden leg (banded in silver) to defy the British fleet—alas, in vain.

There were also Indians who "improved daily and wonderfully by their intercourse with the whites. They . . . learned to cheat, to lie, to swear, to gamble, to quarrel, to cut each other's throats, in short, to excel in all the accomplishments that had originally marked the superiority of their Christian visitors."

Characters, caricatures, solid history, satire—as at a fair or supermarket, there was something for everyone. Some Dutch "first families" reacted as waspishly as William the Testy when they read the volume, but the rest of New York loved it. It was a masterpiece, a best seller that in its first year brought Irving the princely sum of $2,000 in royalties. He was recognized as New York's leading author, and everywhere greeted by name—by the name, that is, of "Diedrich!"

But he could no longer write. Literary fame could not make up for the loss of Matilda.

He tried to force himself by experimenting further with word pictures of the Hudson: "Morning—5 o'clock sky perfectly clear—Sun not up yet a soft mellow yellowish light over the landscape—perfectly calm—river like a glass. In some places almost black from the dark shadows of the mountains . . . long sheets of mist suspended in mid air halfway up the mountains."

Then he gave up even these finger exercises. In 1811, his merchant brothers sent him to Washington to be—of all things!—a lobbyist. They feared that southern politicians representing a "farm bloc" would injure northern commercial interests. Washington Irving accomplished lit-

26

tle except to attend Dolly Madison's gay parties.

Dolly Madison, he wrote a friend, "is a fine, portly buxom dame, who has a smile and a pleasant word for everybody, . . . but as to Jemmy Madison [President Madison]—ah! poor Jemmy! he is but a withered little apple-John."

His letters became flippant, even cynical. He described the beaux and ladies of the capital. One beauty was an "ortolan [bobolink], too rare and costly a dainty for a poor man to afford." Another was "acting very much the part of the Dog in the manger—she cannot enjoy her own chastity but seems unwilling to let any body else do it." A young blade was "a notable leerer at buxom chamber maids and servant girls."

He temporarily recovered from this cynicism when the War of 1812 broke out. Although the war was not popular in the North, there was real anxiety about a British invasion from Canada. Irving, who almost enlisted at the outset, was stirred to accept a position as editor of the *Analectic Magazine* and to publish biographies of popular American naval heroes in that periodical. He himself wrote a number of these. Then when the publisher of the *Analectic* went bankrupt and the British burned Washington, Irving did enlist, in the New York militia.

He was sent to the front in upper New York, as aide-de-camp under General Daniel Tompkins. But the fighting there died away as the British concentrated on the siege of New Orleans. Then the war ended on February 15, 1815.

What should he do now? He was "weary of every thing and of myself." A wartime friend, gallant Stephen Decatur, invited Irving to join a naval expedition against the pirates of Algeria.

Why not? Washington Irving packed his trunks and stowed them on Decatur's ship. Then Napoleon escaped from the island of Elba, and Decatur's departure was delayed because of the turmoil in the Mediterranean. But Washington did not want to wait—he had felt a faint lift of his spirits at the thought of Europe.

His brother Peter, in charge of the Liverpool branch of the family business, was in ill health. Very well—he would sail to England to help Peter.

"I determined . . . to break off . . . from idle habits . . . and when I returned to settle myself down to useful and honourable application," Washington Irving resolved.

He said farewell to his aging mother, and sailed on May 25, 1815. A few weeks later he was lodged with his sister Sarah and her husband, a cheerful businessman who had settled in Birmingham, Henry Van Wart. Surrounded by bright-eyed nephews and nieces, Washington was happier than he had been for years.

With an American friend, he now made a "Grand Welsh tour" and wrote descriptions of the inns and the countryside: "I was shown into a low parlor, lighted by a latticed window and furnished with old oak chairs and tables polished to the utmost brightness. [Here was a] sportsman . . . of a florid complexion; with a hooked nose, prominent chin, and an obliquity of eye."

But Washington's vacation was soon over. In Liverpool he found Peter crippled by rheumatism and the business failing. Peter had bought too much English hardware to ship to America at a time when America had a surplus of such goods. Prices were falling. And bad weather delayed the shipment of these goods, so no money came back, even from lower sales.

Washington Irving worked over the accounts until his eyes were red.

"There it was, day after day," he wrote. "Work hard all day and then to bed late, a troubled sleep, for three hours perhaps, and then wake up; thump, thump, thump, at the heart comes the care. No more sleep for that night. . . .

Wind due east, due east, day after day, no ship can come in, payments must be made, and nowhere for remittances to come from."

By mid-1817 the firm of Peter and Ebenezer Irving had gone under, although bankruptcy proceedings would not be completed until March, 1818.

"I underwent ruin in all its bitterness and humiliation," wrote Washington, "in a strange land—among strangers. . . . I shut myself up from society—and would see no one."

Then he received news of his mother's death in New York.

Washington Irving had arrived at the second great crisis of his life. Grieving for his mother, he also faced the prospect of not knowing where his next meal would come from. Always, before, his brothers had thrown him a lifeline from the profits of the family business.

His savings would last only a short while. He had forgotten what little knowledge of the law he had ever acquired. What *could* he take up?

"The idea suddenly came to return to my pen," he said. "Not so much for support, for bread and water had no terrors for me, but to reinstate myself in the world's thoughts —to raise myself from the degradation into which I considered myself fallen. I took my resolution—threw myself a stranger into London, shut myself up and went to work."

"*I . . . shut myself up and went to work.*" This decision to become a full-time writer was a turning point in Washington Irving's life. It was a lasting commitment, for he was to refuse the position of chief clerk in the Washington Navy Department, offered him just a year later.

After working a few weeks in the London heat, he journeyed to Scotland, in search of the secrets of authorship. He carried a letter to Sir Walter Scott, given him by the English poet Thomas Campbell, about whom Irving had once written an essay.

29

When he reached Abbotsford, Scott's restored medieval abbey, he was welcomed by a powerfully built man in an old green shooting coat and battered white hat.

"Ye're just in time for breakfast, and afterward ye shall see all the wonders of the Abbey!" cried Scott.

The hours flew by while Scott and Irving rode over the bare Scottish hills or sat before a blazing fire. Scott had laughed at Irving's *History of New York* until his "sides [were] absolutely sore." Now he urged Washington to continue with the study of German folklore Washington had recently begun. Scott's talk was of romantic German legends, of Scottish border ballads, of the supernatural, of the realm of the imagination. "This was to be happy," said Irving when he recalled these conversations.

A visit to his sister Sarah's cheerful Birmingham home further raised his spirits. One evening, after an excited discussion of the old days along the Hudson, he rushed up to his room and wrote all night. By dawn "Rip Van Winkle," based on a German folklore plot from Otmar's *Volkssagen,* was finished.

Soon Washington Irving had put together a *Sketch Book* of thirty-two essays and short stories. In addition to "simple good-natured" Rip Van Winkle with his "fowling-piece" and his "termagant wife," there was Ichabod Crane—"tall, but exceedingly lank, with narrow shoulders, long arms and legs, hands that dangled a mile out of his sleeves, feet that might have served for shovels." "The Legend of Sleepy Hollow," Ichabod's story, was matched by a Gothic ghost story, "The Spectre Bridegroom." Among the essays, "Christmas" described the English Yule log; "Stratford-on-Avon" conducted the reader through Shakespeare's home-town; "Westminster Abbey" showed him the tombs of kings and the transitoriness of life.

Here was all the humor of Irving's early writings, tinged with a new romantic sentiment which perhaps came from his suffering. Washington Irving again adopted a pseudonym: The author of these "sketches" would appear as Geoffrey Crayon. They were published first in installments in America (1819–1820), then complete in England (1820).

"In the four quarters of the globe, who reads an American book?" asked the English critic Sydney Smith—an ill-timed question.

The English reviewers answered him. "Crayon," declared Lord Byron, the literary lion of Europe, "is very good." "*The Sketch Book*—is a timid, beautiful work. . . . The touches of poetry are everywhere," said the authoritative *Blackwood's*. "It proves," said the equally authoritative *Edinburgh Magazine,* "that there is *mind* working in America."

Washington Irving found himself famous. He was introduced to the leading literary men, and women, of London. With his brother Peter he journeyed to Paris, where he became friends with the Irish poet Thomas Moore. But he became restless again. He went to work on another book, about "Squire Bracebridge" and the young people of an English manor. (Three-fourths of *The Sketch Book* had been set in England, too.) *Bracebridge Hall,* fifty-one pieces, came out in 1822.

Bracebridge Hall, said the critics, did "not possess the spirit of *The Sketch Book*" but had "redeeming beauties," especially "elegance" of style. Like *The Sketch Book,* it sold well. However, the fact was, Washington Irving had about used up his enthusiasm for merrie England. He needed a new subject, and he found it in the romantic castles of the Rhine.

He now toured Austria and Germany and delighted in the scenery. In his journal he jotted: "Old castle that looks down upon the little village owls hooting on it . . . cottages of village of wood and plaster . . . stream through village

— Walk on bridge of wood—moonlight amphitheatre of black hills—dark firs—forges at distance."

In November, 1822, he arrived in Dresden, then a tiny German principality. He was welcomed as a distinguished author and found an English family, the Fosters, who made him feel at home—in the kind of warm family circle Washington Irving always seemed to need.

At the Fosters' he passed many evenings, "spent in varied, animated, intelligent . . . conversation, with now and then . . . a song, and now and then a recollection from some favorite author . . . given with beaming looks and beaming eyes."

The beaming eyes were Emily Foster's. She was eighteen and beautiful—also, says a modern scholar, "cultivated, witty, sensitive, serious, and sincere, with a taste for writing, books, music, painting, and the theater." She admired the forty-year-old Irving and acted in amateur plays with him. But when Washington fell in love with her and proposed, she rejected him.

This was not a passion as deep as Irving's for Matilda. The experience did not have a lifelong influence upon him. But he was depressed. He journeyed with the Foster family to Rotterdam, and Emily, in *her* journal, wrote a troubled description of their parting:

"Mr. Irving accompanied us down the river quite into the sea, when he was put down into the boat, as he looked up to us, so pale and melancholy, I thought I never felt a more painful moment, such starts of regret, a little self-reproach and feelings too quick to analyze."

Now Irving completed the book he had been getting up at 5 A.M. every morning in Dresden to write: *Tales of a Traveller,* published in 1824. These were ghost stories, yarns about his beloved banditti, tales of haunted castles, footsteps in the dark, supernatural happenings. But the

critics condemned it as lacking in "invention," overly sentimental, and even indecent (!). One called it " 'STORIES
FOR CHILDREN' by *a Baby Six Feet High!*" And Irving
had thought it was his best book.

Two rejections in a little more than a year! What did it
matter that his overall reputation was intact? That he was
considered not only an established author, but a very eligi-
ble bachelor? Rumor connected him with the former
French Empress Maria Louisa. The poet Shelley's widow
"longed for friendship" with him.

None of this helped. His spirits fell, he was in the dol-
drums—he needed a new impulse in order to carry on his
career. He wrote some essays critical of America; then he
decided they were too critical and destroyed them. He tried
studying Spanish. He lost money on investments.

"Behold the sweetness and freshness and fragrance of
life is over; what remains is seared and withered, and
colorless," he wrote, feeling sorry for himself.

Then, from an unexpected quarter, something stirred.
A startled Irving noted in his journal for January 30,
1826: "Received letter from Mr. Everett, attaching me to
Embassy at Madrid. Inclosing passport and proposing my
translating voyage of Columbus."

Alexander Everett, head of the American legation in
Spain and literary enthusiast, wanted Irving to translate an
important recent work on Columbus. To entice him to
Spain, he had made this offer of a position in the embassy.

Irving stared at the letter. A new subject, a new setting
—as a boy, had he not dreamed of voyaging with the dis-
coverers, of campaigning with the conquistadors?

Suddenly, his imagination was darting ahead. There was
no need for delay. He reviewed his Spanish verbs as he
packed.

"I am on the wing for Madrid!" he cried.

CASTLES IN SPAIN

With his faithful brother Peter at his side, Washington Irving jolted across the Pyrenees in a mule-drawn coach. On over the bleak plain of Castile to "old, barbaric" Madrid, with its colorful population of 150,000, its churches, convents, court, and intrigues.

The mules were hauling Irving into a new period in his literary career. He determined to seek what he later called "massive materials, which form a foundation" for a writer's reputation. These were at hand in the Columbus project.

The light satire of *Salmagundi* was behind him. So was the romantic sentiment of his recent stories and essays—at least, he was abandoning those forms. He entered his third and final period now: the writing of popular biography and history.

Alexander Everett introduced Irving to Obadiah Rich, the American consul who owned a treasure trove of Hispano-American books and documents. Soon Washington Irving was immured as a lodger in the congenial Rich's house, practicing his Spanish with Rich's Spanish wife and beginning the translation expected of him. This was of Martín Fernández de Navarrete's *Colección de los viages y descubrimientos,* a monumental work of scholarship containing the most important documents for Columbus' discovery, including the Admiral's own journal.

But should the renowned Geoffrey Crayon descend to being a mere translator? And also, would a translation of this scholarly work sell? Irving sounded out the publishers and found that "they fear it may be *dry.*"

A bad omen! Especially since Irving himself agreed with the booksellers. So he changed his plan at the start and went to work on an original life of Columbus. It would be based, of course, on Navarrete's documents.

"I have been occupied incessantly with my work," Irving wrote, after some months. "Sometimes all day and a great part of the night in defiance of all the rules I had set myself and at the risk of my health. I never worked so hard, nor so constantly for such a length of time."

A young admirer of Irving, Henry Wadsworth Longfellow, dropped in but was not particularly welcome.

"Sit down," said Washington Irving. "I will talk with you in a moment, but I must first finish this sentence."

The Life and Voyages of Christopher Columbus, published in 1828, was an immediate success with readers and critics. It was factual, solid, readable—in fact, it read like a novel. Columbus was a sympathetic hero, a "man of sensibility" struggling for recognition from benighted courtiers and churchmen. Isabella was a "delicate female," gracious and high-minded. History was a tapestry, woven by the *colorista* (colorer) Irving.

For half a century Irving's masterpiece remained the major work on Columbus in English. Once more Washington had proved himself. He could relax, and in his relief dash off a lighter work, *The Conquest of Granada* (1829), the story of the capture of the last Moorish stronghold in Spain.

In 1828 he traveled south to Granada. When he reached the city, with its famous Moorish fortress, the Alhambra, his letter to a friend sang:

"Granada, *bellissima* Granada! . . . we turned a promontory . . . and Granada, with its towers, its Alhambra, and its snowy mountains, burst upon our sight. The evening sun shone gloriously upon its red towers as we approached it, and gave a mellow tone to the rich scenery of the vega. It was like the magic glow which poetry and romance have shed over this enchanting place."

Washington Irving remained here for more than a year. In January, 1829, he received news that he had been elected a member of the Real Academia de la Historia

(The Royal Academy of History), only the second American to be so honored. And shortly after that he went to live for four months in the romantic Alhambra itself.

There he wandered through the "open courts, with fountains and flowers, where there is every thing assembled to delight the senses, yet where there is not a living being to be seen." He became intimate with the peasant family caretakers—"bright-eyed . . . Dolores . . . a tall stuttering lad who works in the garden named Pepe" and, above all, "my ragged philosopher Mateo." Mateo was Irving's guide, "a kind and simple creature, full of good-will"—and of stories and legends.

Clearly, the Alhambra demanded a book. Washington Irving had already begun a collection of essays and stories about the heroic Spanish-Moorish past. Now he continued it, with vivid portraits of Mateo and his family, descriptions of the courts and fountains, and more tales.

When published, in 1832, *The Alhambra* would become an immediate best seller. It marks Irving's return, for the last time, to the pure romantic style. Indeed, it is the most romantic of all Washington Irving's works, brilliantly colored and unified by a wistful melancholy of days gone by.

"In old times, many hundred years ago, there was a Moorish king named Aben Habuz" begins a typical story, the "Legend of the Arabian Astrologer." Although no one selection is the equal of "Rip Van Winkle" or "The Legend of Sleepy Hollow," this Spanish *Sketch Book* is worthy of the phrase the Moorish poets used to describe the fortress itself: "A pearl set in emeralds."

Could *The Alhambra* have been an even better book? Could Irving have given its characters the unforgettable qualities of an Ichabod Crane or a Wouter Van Twiller? Here is another question which cannot be answered. Washington Irving was in the midstream of his inspiration, composing *The Alhambra,* when an interruption came. In July,

1829, he was offered an important position as secretary of the American legation in London.

Although he had been well paid for his books for the last ten years, this position offered greater security still. Would his writing suffer? *Could* he wrench himself away from these peaceful Moorish courts?

Washington wrote desperately to Peter asking for advice. He agonized, for three days. Then he sent his reply. He accepted the post.

Once more he packed, and it was like waking from a dream. The cloud castles of romance had vanished. Goodbye to Dolores, to Pepe, to Mateo. He would round off *The Alhambra* in London, amid the down-to-earth realities of diplomacy and politics. . . .

He spent three years in London, working hard and renewing some old friendships. Then he embarked, for the first time in seventeen years, on a ship headed west. New York lay just over the horizon.

HOMECOMING

"[I] descried the land," Washington Irving described his arrival to three hundred fellow citizens, honoring him at a public dinner in New York's City Hall. "A thousand sails of all descriptions gleaming along the horizon . . . populous villages . . . a forest of masts . . . a fair city and stately harbour."

It was May 30, 1832. He had been back just over a week. Overcome with genuine emotion, he now answered a question as to how long he would remain.

"As long as I live!"

During Irving's absence, there had been many changes. The East River, as he had noted, was crowded with ships from overseas. He wondered at the rows of substantial brick and stone houses, trimmed with marble, which now

37

sheltered New York's population of nearly 250,000. He found the latest maps crisscrossed with the lines of new roads and canals. If he could have joined a flock of migrating birds, he would have looked down, as far west as Arkansas, on freshly cleared fields still dotted with blackened stumps. Commerce was king. The leisurely eighteenth-century life-style of his boyhood was fast disappearing, and all was hustle, westward expansion, and money getting.

Washington Irving did not altogether approve of these changes, but he did not publicly criticize them—he would not be a "creaking door." Earlier the boom helped propel his brother William into Congress and his brother John into a judgeship.

This tumultuous new America had welcomed him as its outstanding author and was further honoring him with "Knickerbocker" hotels, "Knickerbocker" cigars, and "Knickerbocker" steamboats. America's energy *was* exhilarating.

For a time Washington Irving caught the fever. He must travel west, must collect material for a book about his own country. From a steamboat he made the following observations:

"Evening scene on Ohio—Steam boat aground with two flats each side of her. We take part of cargo on board—moonlight—light of fires—chant and chorus of negro boat men—men strolling about docks with cigars negroes dancing before furnaces glassy surface of River—undulations made by boat wavering light of moon and stars."

Incidentally, although Irving was critical of black people, he was a strong antislavery man. He was in South Carolina in 1832, when there was much talk of secession, and the governor urged him to visit the state again.

"Oh, yes," replied Washington Irving. "I'll come with *the first troops!*"

He now wrote three books about the West. *A Tour on*

the Prairies (in *The Crayon Miscellany,* 1835) was a bright watercolor of the frontier, full of anecdotes and scenes like that in the journal entry above. It was very popular among his countrymen.

Astoria (1836) and *Captain Bonneville, U.S.A.* (1837) were about the development of the fur trade beyond the Rockies. The Wall Street developer John Jacob Astor asked Irving to write *Astoria,* and *Captain Bonnevile, U.S.A.* was a sequel to it. Irving romanticized Astor's exploitation of the West and was denounced by some critics, especially James Fenimore Cooper, for not denouncing Astor. Both books sold well, and in addition, Astor paid an undisclosed sum for *Astoria.*

But these books were, in a sense, unworthy of the Washington Irving of *The Sketch Book* and *The Alhambra.* With his cosmopolitan background, Irving could not identify with the American West as Mark Twain later would —could not immortalize pilots on the Mississippi or a "celebrated jumping frog of Calaveras County."

What would be a suitable subject for him?

In 1838 Irving felt he had found it. Why not tell the truly epic story of Cortes' conquest of Mexico? Of the capture of Montezuma and the *Noche Triste* (Sad Night) of the Spanish retreat? He would depict the Aztec temples, the stone platforms of human sacrifice, the brilliant featherwork of the artisans—would describe the snowclad mountains, the canoe-covered Lake Texcoco—for the first time in English!

Washington Irving plunged into libraries. He made a plan for the entire work. One day, in the New York Society Library, he encountered a friend of the young New England historian of Spain, William Prescott. Something aroused Irving's suspicions.

"Is Mr. Prescott engaged on an American subject?" Irving asked.

"Yes," the gentleman replied.

"What is it?" Irving hesitated. "Is it—the conquest of Mexico?"

"Yes," was the answer. "That is his subject."

Irving's heart sank. For reasons that have never been known, he immediately gave up his project in favor of the younger man, who would eventually produce a classic. Then he went home and out into his garden, where he "took to planting cabbages most desperately."

The garden was at Sunnyside, Irving's name for the "neglected cottage" on the Hudson which he had remodeled. It was near Tarrytown, a few miles up the river, his first permanent home. He described it as "a little old fashioned stone mansion, all made up of gable ends, and as full of angles and corners as an old cocked hat."

He had settled here with Peter and one of their nieces, Sarah Paris, in 1836. When Peter died, in 1838, work on the conquest of Mexico would have helped Irving get over the loss of his brother. But he was a professional—he would find another subject.

His reputation had never been higher. It "flourishes greenly in two hemispheres," proclaimed the *United States Magazine*. Englishmen considered him one of the two most interesting aspects of American life, the other being Niagara Falls. This was a little disconcerting.

It was more flattering that Longfellow, Hawthorne, and Poe all were eager students of his style. But these young men were creating a different, more intellectual literature. "Irving," Poe said, "heads the school of the *quietists*."

He tried his hand at a sentimental biography, of an American poetess whose life was cut short, Margaret Miller Davidson, published in 1841. It was popular, yet Irving recognized its shortcomings.

"Oh! if I could only have a 'run of luck,' " he exclaimed.

He looked over some notes for a biography of George

40

Washington, made in 1825. Just as he might have been reaching out toward this major theme, the United States government placed something different in his hand.

"Washington Irving will be the most astonished man in New York," said Daniel Webster, the instigator of the affair.

On February 10, 1842, in New York, Washington Irving learned that he had just been appointed ambassador to Spain.

AMBASSADOR OF LETTERS

"[Washington Irving] was the first ambassador whom the New World of Letters sent to the Old," said the English novelist William Makepeace Thackeray.

From 1842 to 1846, however, Washington Irving was a genuine representative of his government, not of "Letters." He abandoned the journal which he had started on the voyage across. Indeed, says a modern scholar, he came close to giving up the "changeless world of literature" and becoming merely another "prosperous American who wrote occasionally."

For he was delighted with his appointment. His now somewhat stocky figure, neatly clad in the claret-colored coats he favored, was always to be seen in the corridors of the massive Royal Palace of Madrid. He was much happier here than he had been at a public dinner with the English novelist Charles Dickens, whom he found "outrageously vulgar," just before leaving New York.

He had a romantic admiration for Isabella II, "the little queen," whom he described to his sister Catherine:

"She is nearly twelve years of age . . . has a somewhat fair complexion; quite pale, with bluish or light grey eyes; a grave demeanour but a graceful deportment. I could not but regard her with deep interest, knowing . . . to what a

41

stormy and precarious career she might be destined."

He called on the other foreign diplomats to demand sanctuary for "this fragile little being" when Madrid was besieged by rebels. Yet he at once recognized the new revolutionary government after it took over and was on good terms with its head, Ramón Narváez. His books about their country (one-third of all he wrote) had made Washington Irving popular with all Spaniards.

Irving was also respected in England. Now, in an international crisis, the American embassy in London summoned him from Spain. The United States and England were about to go to war over the disputed Oregon boundary. Washington Irving's arrival in London caused the anti-American agitators to lower their voices; negotiators of the two countries then met in a friendly atmosphere and agreed on a compromise.

Back in Madrid, Irving, although he personally disliked the Mexican War, made a strong defense of America's actions to the Spanish government. In 1846 his appointment expired, and he returned to Sunnyside.

No, he told some New York politicians, he would not be a candidate for mayor of their city. Why, he demanded of his nephew Pierre Irving, must there be that infernal "screeching" of locomotives in the Hudson valley? Then, made comfortable by Pierre and his nieces, he picked up his pen and returned to his lifelong constituency, the "New World of Letters."

"I have never found, in anything outside of the four walls of my study, any enjoyment equal to sitting at my writing desk with a clean page, a new theme, and a mind wide awake," he said.

At sixty-three, he turned out some miscellaneous, yet substantial writings, including biographies of Oliver Goldsmith and Mahomet. He had begun the biographies earlier, but finishing them at his age was an accomplishment.

Finally, he took up his materials on George Washington and decided to end his career with a major study of his first hero. In 1851 he set off on a new round of researches: newspapers in Baltimore; government records and military dispatches in Washington; a study of the rooms, furniture, and gardens of Mount Vernon; a survey of the scene of Burgoyne's surrender at Saratoga.

"I live only in the Revolution," said the gray-haired Irving. "I have no other existence now—can think of nothing else."

George Washington's character, he admitted, at first "suggested the idea of a statue; however you might admire it, you could not embrace it. But as I became better acquainted with the real life of the man, his constant untiring benevolence, I loved him more and more."

When the five volumes were finished, the historian Prescott thought Irving had succeeded in making Washington "a being of flesh and blood, like ourselves." Other contemporaries agreed that Irving had achieved his goal of presenting "the facts in the most lucid order." His *Life of Washington,* solidly based on Jared Sparks' *Life and Writings of Washington* and less sentimental than its competitors, would be the most widely read biography for the rest of the century.

Nevertheless, writing it was backbreaking toil for an author in his seventies. Washington Irving still found time for walks and drives and was active in the Tarrytown Episcopal Church, but his health was failing.

"I am getting ready to go," he said. "I am shutting up my doors and windows."

On March 15, 1859, he handed the last chapter of the last volume of *Washington* to his nephew Pierre "and sank exhausted on the red sofa."

"I must weave my web and then die," he had said earlier of this self-imposed final assignment.

Well, he had done it, and more. He had written the great shelfful of books he had dreamed of so long ago. There they stood, in the twilight—stout *Knickerbocker, The Sketch Book, Bracebridge Hall, The Life and Voyages of Christopher Columbus,* the *Conquest of Granada, The Alhambra,* and a dozen others, side by side with *Robinson Crusoe* and *Sinbad the Sailor* for all the years to come.

Now he would rest.

When Washington Irving died on November 28, 1859, his position as the first American man of letters was secure. He had proved that an American could write well. He had made history as interesting as fiction, by emphasizing characters and pageantry.

But he had excelled in the short story and essay. His forty-five stories, one-third of them based on German sources, popularized the romantic tale in America. As for the essay, his likable personality suited this form perfectly. Who would not be eager to read on in a book which started like the *Sketch Book:* "I was always fond of visiting new scenes, and observing strange characters and manners"?

He had succeeded in part because of a style which appeared "natural" and "easy" but was the result of such hard work revising. He gained this clarity by "shaking . . . superfluous words out of the sentences, which weaken them."

"I want the action to shine through the style," he said. "No style, indeed; no encumbrance of ornament."

"I consider a story merely as a frame on which to stretch my materials," he wrote elsewhere. "It is the play of thought, and sentiment, and language; the weaving in of characters lightly, yet expressively, delineated; the familiar and faithful exhibition of scenes in common life; and the half-concealed vein of humor that is often playing through the whole;—these are among what I aim at."

It was not Irving's function "either to scale the heights or sound the depths of life," observes a modern critic. This is true. Washington Irving offered only superb entertainment, humor, good manners—"a good deal of what we generally mean to indicate when we speak of civilization."

Perhaps this is not much, weighed in the scales against passion, violence, exorcism, and other themes popular in the twentieth century. But for more than a hundred and fifty years it has been enough—enough, that is, to attract millions of readers.

It is likely to continue to attract them. For in the pages written by the dreamer who used to flee across his roof to the John Street Theater one can still escape to a Granada, a Stratford, or a Sleepy Hollow where "every thing [is] fairy land." This is the legacy of Washington Irving, America's "Ambassador of Letters" to people of all nations, around the world.

The Characters of
WASHINGTON IRVING

Washington Irving wrote essays, short stories, biography, and history. But whatever form he took up, it is his characters that live. The reader recalls Rip Van Winkle trudging up the Hudson, ancient fowling piece in hand, while Dame Van Winkle's complaints echo shrilly behind. He visualizes the "small, elderly gentleman, dressed in an old black coat and cocked hat" resting by the road to Albany, clutching "a small bundle tied in a red bandana handkerchief"—Diedrich Knickerbocker. He remembers wily Ferdinand and saintly Isabella—and "the renowned Wouter Van Twiller" stolidly watching "the smoke curling from his pipe to the ceiling"—and a host of others.

Characters are Washington Irving's legacy to America. One, Diedrich Knickerbocker, has bestowed his name on the nation's largest city. Several have become legends. The following selections present sketches of some of the best known.

RIP VAN WINKLE

Whoever has made a voyage up the Hudson must remember the Kaatskill mountains. They are a dismembered branch of the great Appalachian family, and are seen away to the west of the river, swelling up to a noble height, and lording it over the surrounding country. Every change of season, every change of weather, indeed, every hour of the day, produces some change in the magical hues and shapes of these mountains, and they are regarded by all the good wives, far and near, as perfect barometers. When the weather is fair and settled, they are clothed in blue and purple, and print their bold outlines on the clear evening sky; but, sometimes, when the rest of the landscape is cloudless, they will gather a hood of gray vapors about their summits, which, in the last rays of the setting sun, will glow and light up like a crown of glory.

At the foot of these fairy mountains, the voyager may have descried the light smoke curling up from a village, whose shingle-roofs gleam among the trees, just where the blue tints of the upland melt away into the fresh green of the nearer landscape. It is a little village, of great antiquity, having been founded by some of the Dutch colonists, in the early times of the province, just about the beginning of the government of the good Peter Stuyvesant, (may he rest in peace!) and there were some of the houses of the original settlers standing within a few years, built of small yellow bricks brought from Holland, having latticed windows and gable fronts, surmounted with weathercocks.

In that same village, and in one of these very houses (which, to tell the precise truth, was sadly time-worn and weather-beaten), there lived many years since, while the country was yet a province of Great Britain, a simple good-natured fellow, of the name of Rip Van Winkle. He was a descendant of the Van Winkles who figured so gallantly in the chivalrous days of Peter Stuyvesant, and accompanied him to the siege of Fort Christina. He inherited, however, but little of the martial character of his ancestors. I have observed that he was a simple good-natured man; he was, moreover, a kind neighbor, and an obedient hen-pecked husband. Indeed, to the latter circumstance might be owing that meekness of spirit which gained him such universal popularity; for those men are most apt to be obsequious and conciliating abroad, who are under the discipline of shrews at home. Their tempers, doubtless, are rendered pliant and malleable in the fiery furnace of domestic tribulation; and a curtain lecture is worth all the sermons in the world for teaching the virtues of patience and long-suffering. A termagant wife may, therefore, in some respects, be considered a tolerable blessing; and if so, Rip Van Winkle was thrice blessed.

Certain it is, that he was a great favorite among all the good wives of the village, who, as usual, with the amiable sex, took his part in all family squabbles; and never failed, whenever they talked those matters over in their evening gossipings, to lay all the blame on Dame Van Winkle. The children of the village, too, would shout with joy whenever he approached. He assisted at their sports, made them playthings, taught them to fly kites and shoot marbles, and told them long stories of ghosts, witches, and Indians. Whenever he went dodging about the village, he was surrounded by a troop of them, hanging on his skirts, clambering on his back, and playing a thousand tricks on him with impunity; and not a dog would bark at him throughout the neighborhood.

The great error in Rip's composition was an insuperable aversion to all kinds of profitable labor. It could not be from the want of assiduity or perseverance; for he would sit on a wet rock, with a rod as long and heavy as a Tartar's lance, and fish all day without a murmur, even though he should not be encouraged by a single nibble. He would carry a fowling-piece on his shoulder for hours together, trudging through woods and swamps, and up hill and down dale, to shoot a few squirrels or wild pigeons. He would never refuse to assist a neighbor even in the roughest toil, and was a foremost man at all country frolics for husking Indian corn, or building stone-fences; the women of the village, too, used to employ him to run their errands, and to do such little odd jobs as their less obliging husbands would not do for them. In a word Rip was ready to attend to anybody's business but his own; but as to doing family duty, and keeping his farm in order, he found it impossible.

(The Sketch Book)

ICHABOD CRANE

In this by-place of nature, there abode . . . a worthy wight of the name of Ichabod Crane; who sojourned, or, as he expressed it, "tarried," in Sleepy Hollow, for the purpose of instructing the children of the vicinity. He was a native of Connecticut; a State which supplies the Union with pioneers for the mind as well as for the forest, and sends forth yearly its legions of frontier woodsmen and country schoolmasters. The cognomen of Crane was not inapplicable to his person. He was tall, but exceedingly lank, with narrow shoulders, long arms and legs, hands that dangled a mile out of his sleeves, feet that might have served for shovels, and his whole frame most loosely hung together. His head was small, and flat at top, with huge ears, large green glassy eyes, and a long snipe nose, so that it looked like a weather-cock, perched upon his spindle neck, to tell which way the wind blew. To see him striding along the profile of a hill on a windy day, with his clothes bagging and fluttering about him, one might have mistaken him for the genius of famine descending upon the earth, or some scarecrow eloped from a cornfield.

His school-house . . . stood in a rather lonely but pleasant situation, just at the foot of a woody hill, with a brook running close by, and a formidable birch tree growing at one end of it. From hence the low murmur of his pupils' voices, conning over their lessons, might be heard in a drowsy summer's day, like the hum of a bee-hive; interrupted now and then by the authoritative voice of the master, in the tone of menace or command; or, peradventure, by the appalling sound of the birch, as he urged some tardy loiterer along the flowery path of knowledge. Truth to say, he was a conscientious man, and ever bore in mind the golden maxim, "Spare the rod and spoil the child."—Ichabod Crane's scholars certainly were not spoiled.

I would not have it imagined, however, that he was one of those cruel potentates of the school, who joy in the smart of their subjects; on the contrary, he administered justice with discrimination rather than severity. . . .

When school hours were over, he was even the companion and playmate of the larger boys; and on holiday afternoons would convoy some of the smaller ones home, who happened to have pretty sisters, or good housewives for mothers, noted for the comforts of the cupboard. Indeed it behooved him to keep on good terms with his pupils. The revenue arising from his school was small, and would have been scarcely sufficient to furnish him with daily bread, for he was a huge feeder, and though lank, had the dilating powers of an anaconda; but to help out his maintenance, he was, according to country custom in those parts, boarded and lodged at the houses of the farmers, whose children he instructed. With these he lived successively, a week at a time; thus going the rounds of the neighborhood, with all his worldly effects tied up in a cotton handkerchief. . . .

He assisted the farmers occasionally in the lighter labors of their farms; helped to make hay; mended the fences; took the horses to water; drove the cows from pasture; and cut wood for the winter fire. . . . He found favor in the eyes of the mothers, by petting the children, particularly the youngest. . . .

In addition to his other vocations, he was the singing-master of the neighborhood, and picked up many bright shillings by instructing the young folks in psalmody. It was a matter of no little vanity to him, on Sundays, to take his station in front of the church gallery, with a band of chosen singers; where, in his own mind, he completely carried away the palm from the parson. Certain it is, his voice resounded far above all the rest of the congregation; and there are peculiar quavers still to be heard in that church, and which may even be heard half a mile off, quite to the opposite side of the mill-pond, on a still Sunday morning, which are said to be legitimately descended from the nose of Ichabod Crane.

(The Sketch Book)

WOUTER VAN TWILLER

The renowned Wouter (or Walter) Van Twiller, was descended from a long line of Dutch burgomasters, who had successively dozed away their lives, and grown fat upon the bench of magistracy in Rotterdam; and who had comported themselves with such singular wisdom and propriety, that they were never either heard or talked of—which, next to being universally applauded, should be the object of ambition of all magistrates and rulers. There are two opposite ways by which some men make a figure in the world; one by talking faster than they think; and the other by holding their tongues and not thinking at all. By the first, many a smatterer acquires the reputation of a man of quick parts; by the other, many a dunder-pate, like the owl, the stupidest of birds, comes to be considered the very type of wisdom. This, by the way, is a casual remark, which I would not, for the universe, have it thought I apply to Governor Van Twiller. It is true he was a man shut up within himself, like an oyster, and rarely spoke except in monosyllables; but then it was allowed he seldom said a foolish thing. So invincible was his gravity that he was never known to laugh or even to smile through the whole course of a long and prosperous life. Nay if a joke were uttered in his presence, that set light minded hearers in a roar, it was observed to throw him into a state of perplexity. Sometimes he would deign to inquire into the matter, and when, after much explanation, the joke was made as plain as a pike-staff, he would continue to smoke his pipe in silence, and at length, knocking out the ashes would exclaim, "Well! I see nothing in all that to laugh about."

With all his reflective habits, he never made up his mind on a subject. His adherents accounted for this by the astonishing magnitude of his ideas. He conceived every subject on so grand a scale that he had not room in his head to turn it over and examine both sides of it. Certain it is that if any matter were propounded to him on which ordinary mortals would rashly determine at first glance, he would put on a vague, mysterious look; shake his capacious head; smoke some time in profound silence, and at length observe that "he had his doubts about the matter," which gained him the reputation of a man slow of belief and not easily imposed upon. What is more, it gained him a lasting name; for to this habit of the mind has been attributed his surname of Twiller; which is said to be a corruption of the original Twijfler, or, in plain English, *Doubter*.

The person of this illustrious old gentleman was formed and proportioned, as though it had been moulded by the hands of some cunning Dutch statuary, as a model of majesty and lordly grandeur. He was exactly five feet six inches in height, and six feet five inches in circumference. His head was a perfect sphere, and of such stupendous dimensions, that dame Nature, with all her sex's ingenuity, would have been puzzled to construct a neck capable of supporting it; wherefore she wisely declined the attempt, and settled it firmly on the top of his back bone, just between the shoulders. His body was oblong and particularly capacious at bottom; which was wisely ordered by Providence, seeing that he was a man of sedentary habits, and very averse to the idle labor of walking. His legs were short, but sturdy in proportion to the weight they had to sustain; so that when erect he had not a little the appearance of a beer barrel on skids. His face, that infallible index of the mind, presented a vast expanse, unfurrowed by any of those lines and angles which disfigure the human countenance with what is termed expression. Two small grey eyes twinkled feebly in the midst, like two stars of lesser magnitude in a hazy firmament; and his full-fed cheeks, which seemed to have taken toll of every thing that went into his mouth, were curiously mottled and streaked with dusky red, like a spitzenberg apple.

His habits were as regular as his person. He daily took his four stated meals, appropriating exactly an hour to each; he smoked and doubted eight hours, and he slept the remaining twelve of the four and twenty. Such was the renowned Wouter Van Twiller—a true philosopher, for his mind was either elevated above, or tranquilly settled below, the cares and perplexities of this world. He had lived in it for years, without feeling the least curiosity to know whether the sun revolved round it, or it round the sun; and he had watched, for at least half a century, the smoke curling from his pipe to the ceiling, without once troubling his head with any of those numerous theories, by which a philosopher would have perplexed his brain, in accounting for its rising above the surrounding atmosphere.

In his council he presided with great state and solemnity. He sat in a huge chair of solid oak, hewn in the celebrated forest of the Hague, fabricated by an experienced timmerman of Amsterdam, and curiously carved about the arms and feet, into exact imitations of gigantic eagle's claws. Instead of a sceptre he swayed a long Turkish pipe, wrought with jasmine and amber, which had been presented to a stadholder of Holland, at the conclusion of a treaty with one of the petty Barbary powers. In this stately chair would he sit, and his magnificent pipe would he smoke, shaking his right knee with a constant motion, and fixing his eye for hours together upon a little print of Amsterdam, which hung in a black frame against the opposite wall of the council chamber. Nay, it has even been said, that when any deliberation of extraordinary length and intricacy was on the carpet, the renowned Wouter would shut his eyes for full two hours at a time, that he might not be disturbed by external objects—and at such times the internal commotion of his mind was evinced by certain regular guttural sounds, which his admirers declared were merely the noise of conflict, made by his contending doubts and opinions.

(Knickerbocker's History of New York)

WILLIAM THE TESTY

Wilhelmus Kieft, who, in 1634, ascended the gubernatorial chair . . . had not been a year in the government of the province, before he was universally denominated William the Testy. His appearance answered to his name. He was a brisk, wiry, waspish little old gentleman; such a one as may now and then be seen stumping about our city in a broad-skirted coat with huge buttons, a cocked hat stuck on the back of his head, and a cane as high as his chin. His face was broad, but his features were sharp; his cheeks were scorched into a dusky red, by two fiery little gray eyes; his nose turned up, and the corners of his mouth turned down, pretty much like the muzzle of an irritable pug-dog.

I have heard it observed by a profound adept in human physiology, that if a woman waxes fat with the progress of years, her tenure of life is somewhat precarious, but if haply she withers as she grows old, she lives forever. Such promised to be the case with William the Testy, who grew tough in proportion as he dried. He had withered, in fact, not through the process of years, but through the tropical fervor of his soul, which burnt like a vehement rush-light in his bosom; inciting him to incessant broils and bickerings. Ancient traditions speak much of his learning, and of the gallant inroads he had made into the dead languages, in which he had made captive a host of Greek nouns and Latin verbs; and brought off rich booty in ancient saws and apothegms; which he was wont to parade in his public harangues, as a triumphant general of yore, his *spolia opima*. Of metaphysics he knew enough to confound all hearers and himself into the bargain. In logic, he knew the whole family of syllogisms and dilemmas, and was so proud of his skill that he never suffered even a self-evident fact to pass unargued. It was observed, however, that he seldom got into an argument without getting into a perplexity, and then into a passion with his adversary for not being convinced gratis.

He had, moreover, skirmished smartly on the frontiers of several of the sciences, was fond of experimental philosophy, and prided himself upon inventions of all kinds. His abode, which he had fixed at a Bowerie or country-seat at a short distance from the city, just at what is now called Dutch-street, soon abounded with proofs of his ingenuity: patent smokejacks that required a horse to work them; Dutch ovens that roasted meat without fire; carts that went before the horses; weathercocks that turned against the wind; and other wrong-headed contrivances that astonished and confounded all beholders. The house, too, was beset with paralytic cats and dogs, the subjects of his experimental philosophy; and the yelling and yelping of the latter unhappy victims of science, while aiding in the pursuit of knowledge, soon gained for the place the name of "Dog's Misery," by which it continues to be known even at the present day.

It is in knowledge as in swimming; he who flounders and splashes on the surface, makes more noise, and attracts more attention, than the pearl-diver who quietly dives in quest of treasures to the bottom. The vast acquirements of the new governor were the theme of marvel among the simple burghers of New Amsterdam; he figured about the place as learned a man as a Bonze at Pekin, who has mastered one half of the Chinese alphabet: and was unanimously pronounced a "universal genius!"

I have known in my time many a genius of this stamp; but, to speak my mind freely, I never knew one who, for the ordinary purposes of life, was worth his weight in straw. In this respect, a little sound judgment and plain common sense is worth all the sparkling genius that ever wrote poetry or invented theories. Let us see how the universal acquirements of William the Testy aided him in the affairs of government.

(Knickerbocker's History of New York)

THE PIPE PLOT

Wilhelmus Kieft . . . had been greatly annoyed by the factious meeting of the good people of New Amsterdam, but, observing that on these occasions the pipe was ever in their mouth, he began to think that the pipe was at the bottom of the affair, and that there was some mysterious affinity between politics and tobacco smoke. Determined to strike at the root of the evil, he began, forthwith, to rail at tobacco, as a noxious, nauseous weed; filthy in all its uses; and as to smoking he denounced it as a heavy tax upon the public pocket; a vast consumer of time, a great encourager of idleness, and a deadly bane to the prosperity and morals of the people. Finally he issued an edict, prohibiting the smoking of tobacco throughout the New Netherlands.

Ill-fated Kieft! Had he lived in the present age and attempted to check the unbounded license of the press, he could not have struck more sorely upon the sensibilities of the million. The pipe, in fact, was the great organ of reflection and deliberation of the New Netherlander. It was his constant companion and solace—was he gay, he smoked; was he sad, he smoked; his pipe was never out of his mouth; it was a part of his physiognomy; without it his best friends would not know him. Take away his pipe? You might as well take away his nose!

The immediate effect of the edict of William the Testy was a popular commotion. A vast multitude armed with pipes and tobacco-boxes, and an immense supply of ammunition, sat themselves down before the governor's house, and fell to smoking with tremendous violence. The

57

testy William issued forth like a wrathful spider, demanding the reason of this lawless fumigation. The sturdy rioters replied by lolling back in their seats, and puffing away with redoubled fury; raising such a murky cloud that the governor was fain to take refuge in the interior of his castle.

A long negotiation ensued through the medium of Antony the Trumpeter. The governor was at first wrathful and unyielding, but was gradually smoked into terms. He concluded by permitting the smoking of tobacco, but he abolished the fair long pipes used in the days of Wouter Van Twiller, denoting ease, tranquillity, and sobriety of deportment; these he condemned as incompatible with the despatch of business, in place whereof he substituted little captious short pipes, two inches in length, which he observed, could be stuck in one corner of the mouth, or twisted in the hat-band; and would never be in the way. Thus ended this alarming insurrection, which was long known by the name of The Pipe Plot, and which, it has been somewhat quaintly observed, did end, like most plots and seditions, in mere smoke.

But mark, oh, reader! The deplorable evils which did afterwards result. The smoke of these villainous little pipes, continually ascending in a cloud about the nose, penetrated into and befogged the cerebellum; dried up all the kindly moisture of the brain, and rendered the people who used them as vaporish and testy as the governor himself. Nay, what is worse, from being goodly, burly, sleek-conditioned men, they became, like our Dutch yeomanry who smoke short pipes, a lantern-jawed, smoke-dried, leathern-hided race.

Nor was this all. From this fatal schism in tobacco pipes we may date the rise of parties in the Nieuw Nederlands. The rich and self-important burghers who had made their fortunes, and could afford to be lazy, adhered to the ancient fashion, and formed a kind of aristocracy known as the *Long Pipes;* while the lower order, adopting the reform of William Kieft as more convenient in their handicraft employments, were branded with the plebeian name of *Short Pipes.*

A third party sprang up, headed by the descendants of Robert Chewit, the companion of the great Hudson. These discarded pipes altogether and took to chewing tobacco; hence they were called *Quids;* an appellation since given to those political mongrels, which sometimes spring up between two great parties, as a mule is produced between a horse and an ass.

And here I would note the great benefit of party distinctions in saving the people at large the trouble of thinking. Hesiod divides mankind into three classes, those who think for themselves, those who think as others think, and those who do not think at all. The second class comprises the great mass of society; for most people require a set creed and a file-leader. Hence the origin for party: which means a large body of people, some few of whom think, and all the rest talk. The former take the lead and discipline the latter; prescribing what they must say; what they must approve; what they must hoot at; whom they must support; but, above all, whom they must hate; for no one can be a right good partisan, who is not a thoroughgoing hater.

The enlightened inhabitants of the Manhattoes, therefore, being divided into parties, were enabled to hate each other with great accuracy. And now the great business of politics went bravely on, the long pipes and short pipes assembling in separate beer-houses, and smoking at each other with implacable vehemence, to the great support of the state and profit of the tavern-keepers.

(Knickerbocker's History of New York)

59

INDIAN HEROES

In one of the homely narratives of the Indian wars in New England, there is a touching account of the desolation carried into the tribe of the Pequod Indians. Humanity shrinks from the cold-blooded detail of indiscriminate butchery. In one place we read of the surprisal of an Indian fort in the night, when the wigwams were wrapped in flames, and the miserable inhabitants were shot down and slain in attempting to escape, "all being despatched and ended in the course of an hour." After a series of similar transactions, "our soldiers," as the historian piously observes, "being resolved by God's assistance to make a final destruction of them," the unhappy savages being hunted from their homes and fortresses, and pursued with fire and sword, a scanty, but gallant band, the sad remnant of the Pequod warriors, with their wives and children, took refuge in a swamp.

Burning with indignation, and rendered sullen by despair; with hearts bursting with grief at the destruction of their tribe, and spirits galled and sore at the fancied ignominy of their defeat, they refused to ask their lives at the hands of an insulting foe, and preferred death to submission.

As the night drew on they were surrounded in their dismal retreat, so as to render escape impracticable. Thus situated, their enemy "plied them with shot all the time, by which means many were killed and buried in the mire." In the darkness and fog that preceded the dawn of day some few broke through the besiegers and escaped into the woods: "the rest were left to the conquerors, of which many were killed in the swamp, like sullen dogs who would rather, in their self-willedness and madness, sit still and be shot through, or cut to pieces," than implore for mercy.

When the day broke upon this handful of forlorn but dauntless spirits, the soldiers, we are told, entering the swamp, "saw several heaps of them sitting close together, upon whom they discharged their pieces, laden with ten or twelve pistol bullets at a time, putting the muzzles of the pieces under the boughs, within a few yards of them; so as, besides those that were found dead, many more were killed and sunk into the mire, and never were minded more by friend or foe."

Can any one read this plain unvarnished tale, without admiring the stern resolution, the unbending pride, the loftiness of spirit, that seemed to nerve the hearts of these self-taught heroes, and to raise them above the instinctive feelings of human nature? When the Gauls laid waste the city of Rome, they found the senators clothed in their robes, and seated with stern tranquillity in their curule chairs; in this manner they suffered death without resistance or even supplication. Such conduct was, in them, applauded as noble and magnanimous; in the hapless Indian it was reviled as obstinate and sullen! How truly are we the dupes of show and circumstance! How different is virtue, clothed in purple and enthroned in state, from virtue, naked and destitute, and perishing obscurely in a wilderness!

(The Sketch Book)

A STORM IN GERMANY

Mrs. Foster gets on the box [of the coach] with me—fine and warm—country begins to grow more varied—see a storm gathering ahead—it advances rapidly—I see that it is a thunder-gust and likely to be a severe one—get Mrs. Foster into carriage—make the carriage all fast and ready —mount the dicky [driver's seat] with box coat and a fur mantle about my legs, and umbrella—

gust comes on with a hurricane of wind, raising clouds of dust—the earth seems thrown up into the air—the clouds brown with dust—the whole atmosphere thickened and darkened—gust comes more and more terrible—horses can hardly draw on the carriage—

begins to rain—rain driven with incredible violence—hail—large as hazel-nuts—storm increases—one horrible blast of wind succeeds another—umbrella breaks and is whirled off into a neighboring field—mantle flies after it—horses get frightened—

I descend from coach-box—fear the carriage will be blown over—the two leaders become unmanageable—postilion [rider] jumps off and tries to hold them—they turn round and go down a bank—try to keep them quiet—they continue restive—drag carriage after them down a steep bank into a ditch—

pole breaks—carriage overturns—rush to the place and get the ladies out—none hurt materially—bruised a little—drenched to the skin in an instant—

leave them there and run to a house about half a mile off—find a smith's shop with a small country inn beside it—send workmen to look after the carriage, and order rooms to be prepared for ladies—run back to carriage—

the storm is already over—find them all drenched to the skin, but in good spirits and unhurt—they walk to the inn—the carriage is with much trouble righted and dragged up the bank backward by two horses and six or eight men —get safe to the inn—a new pole is made—

we all change our clothes, and after a repast of cold tongue and wine, set off in good spirits—the ladies give their hats, which were quite wet, to a pretty maid servant at the inn—and likewise a shawl—she will be the belle of the neighborhood.

(*A Journal,* 1823)

SIR WALTER SCOTT

In a little while the "lord of the castle" himself [Sir Walter Scott] made his appearance. I knew him at once by the descriptions I had read and heard, and the likenesses that had been published of him. He was tall, and of a large and powerful frame. His dress was simple, and almost rustic. An old green shooting-coat, with a dog-whistle at the button hole, brown linen pantaloons, stout shoes that tied at the ankles, and a white hat that had evidently seen service. He came limping up the gravel walk, aiding himself by a stout walking-staff, but moving rapidly and with vigor. By his side jogged along a large iron-gray stag hound of most grave demeanor, who took no part in the clamor of the canine rabble, but seemed to consider himself bound, for the dignity of the house, to give me a courteous reception.

Before Scott had reached the gate he called out in a hearty tone, welcoming me to Abbotsford, and asking news of Campbell. Arrived at the door of the chaise, he grasped me warmly by the hand: "Come, drive down, drive down to the house," said he, "ye're just in time for breakfast, and afterwards ye shall see all the wonders of the Abbey."

I would have excused myself, on the plea of having already made my breakfast. "Hout, man," cried he, "a ride in the morning in the keen air of the Scotch hills is warrant enough for a second breakfast."

I was accordingly whirled to the portal of the cottage, and in a few moments found myself seated at the breakfast table. There was no one present but the family, which consisted of Mrs. Scott, her eldest daughter Sophia, then a fine girl about seventeen, Miss Ann Scott, two or three years younger, Walter, a well-grown stripling, and Charles, a lively boy, eleven or twelve years of age. I soon felt myself quite at home, and my heart in a glow with the cordial welcome I experienced. I had thought to make a mere morning visit, but found I was not to be let off so lightly.

"You must not think our neighborhood is to be read in a morning, like a newspaper," said Scott. "It takes several days of study for an observant traveller that has a relish for auld world trumpery. After breakfast you shall make your visit to Melrose Abbey; I shall not be able to accompany you, as I have some household affairs to attend to, but I will put you in charge of my son Charles. . . . When you come back, I'll take you out on a ramble about the neighborhood. To-morrow we will take a look at the Yarrow, and the next day we will drive over to Dryburgh Abbey, which is a fine old ruin well worth your seeing"—in a word, before Scott had got through with his plan, I found myself committed for a visit of several days, and it seemed as if a little realm of romance was suddenly opened before me.

(Abbotsford)

FERDINAND AND ISABELLA

Ferdinand was of the middle stature, well proportioned, and hardy and active from athletic exercise. His carriage was free, erect, and majestic. He had a clear, serene forehead, which appeared more lofty from his head being partly bald. His eyebrows were large and parted, and, like his hair, of a bright chestnut; his eyes were clear and animated; his complexion was somewhat ruddy and scorched by the toils of war; his mouth moderate, well formed, and gracious in its expression; his teeth white, though small and irregular; his voice sharp; his speech quick and fluent. His genius was clear and comprehensive; his judgment grave and certain. He was simple in dress and diet, equable in his temper, devout in his religion, and so indefatigable in business that it was said he seemed to repose himself by working. He was a great observer and judge of men, and unparalleled in the science of the cabinet.

Such is the picture given of him by the Spanish historians of his time. It has been added, however, that he had more of bigotry than religion; that his ambition was craving rather than magnanimous; that he made war less like a paladin than a prince, less for glory than for mere dominion; and that his policy was cold, selfish, and artful. He was called the wise and prudent in Spain; in Italy, the pious; in France and England, the ambitious and perfidious. He certainly was one of the most subtle statesmen, but one of the most thorough egotists, that ever sat upon a throne.

Isabella . . . is one of the purest and most beautiful characters in the pages of history. She was well formed, of the middle size, with great dignity and gracefulness of deportment, and a mingled gravity and sweetness of demeanor. Her complexion was fair; her hair auburn, inclining to red; her eyes were of a clear blue, with a benign expression, and there was a singular modesty in her countenance, gracing, as it did a wonderful firmness of purpose, and earnestness of spirit.

Though strongly attached to her husband, and studious of his fame, yet she always maintained her distinct rights as an allied prince. She exceeded him in beauty, in personal dignity, in acuteness of genius, and in grandeur of soul. Combining the active and resolute qualities of man with the softer charities of woman, she mingled in the warlike councils of her husband, engaged personally in his enterprises, and in some instances surpassed him in the firmness and intrepidity of her measures; while, being inspired with a truer idea of glory, she infused a more lofty and generous temper into his subtle and calculating policy.

(The Life and Voyages of Christopher Columbus)

SONS OF THE ALHAMBRA

The Alhambra is in a rapid state of . . . transition. Whenever a tower falls to decay, it is seized upon by some tatterdemalion family, who become joint-tenants, with the bats and owls, of its gilded halls; and hang their rags, those standards of poverty, out of its windows and loop-holes.

I have amused myself with remarking some of the motley characters that have thus usurped the ancient abode of royalty, and who seem as if placed here to give a farcical termination to the drama of human pride. One of these even bears the mockery of a regal title. It is a little old woman named Maria Antonia Sabonea, but who goes by the appellation of *la Reyna Coquina,* or the Cockle-queen. She is small enough to be a fairy; and a fairy she may be for aught I can find out, for no one seems to know her origin.

Her habitation is a kind of closet under the outer staircase of the palace, and she sits in the cool stone corridor, plying her needle and singing from morning till night, with a ready joke for every one that passes; for though one of the poorest, she is one of the merriest little women breathing. Her great merit is a gift for story-telling, having, I verily believe, as many stories at her command as the inexhaustible Scheherazade of the Thousand and One Nights. . . . Notwithstanding her being very little, very ugly, and very poor she has had, according to her own account, five husbands and a half, reckoning as a half one a young dragoon, who died during courtship.

A rival personage to this little fairy queen is a portly old fellow with a bottle-nose, who goes about in a rusty garb, with a cocked hat of oilskin and a red cockade. He is one of the legitimate sons of the Alhambra, and has lived here all his life, filling various offices, such as deputy alguazil, sexton of the parochial church, and marker of a fives-court established at the foot of one of the towers. He is as poor as a rat, but as proud as he is ragged, boasting of his descent from the illustrious house of Aguilar, from which sprang Gonzalvo of Cordova, the grand captain. Nay, he actually bears the name of Alonzo de Aguilar, so renowned in the history of the Conquest; though the graceless wags of the fortress have given him the title of *el padre santo,* or the holy father, the usual appellation of the Pope. . . .

Of this motley community, I find the family of my gossiping squire, Mateo Ximenes, to form, from their numbers at least, a very important part. His boast of being a son of the Alhambra is not unfounded. His family has inhabited the fortress ever since the time of the Conquest, handing down an hereditary poverty from father to son. . . . His father, by trade a ribbon-weaver, and who succeeded the historical tailor as the head of the family, is now near seventy years of age, and lives in a hovel of reeds and plaster, built by his own hands, just above the iron gate. The furniture consists of a crazy bed, a table, and two or three chairs; a wooden chest, containing, besides his scanty clothing, the "archives of the family." These are nothing more nor less than the papers of various lawsuits . . . most of the suits . . . brought against gossiping neighbors for questioning the purity of their blood, and denying their being *Christianos viejos,* i.e. old Christians, without Jewish or Moorish taint. In fact, I doubt whether this jealousy about their blood has not kept them so poor in purse. . . .

As to Mateo himself, who is now about thirty-five years of age, he has done his utmost to perpetuate his line and continue the poverty of the family, having a wife and a numerous progeny, who inhabit an almost dismantled hovel in the hamlet. How they manage to subsist, He only who sees into all mysteries can tell; the subsistence of a Spanish family of the kind is always a riddle to me; yet they do subsist, and what is more, appear to enjoy their existence. The wife takes her holiday stroll on the Paseo of Granada, with a child in her arms and half a dozen at her heels; and the eldest daughter, now verging into womanhood, dresses her hair with flowers, and dances gaily to the castanets.

There are two classes of people to whom life seems one long holiday—the very rich and the very poor; one, because they need do nothing; the other, because they have nothing to do; but there are none who understand the art of doing nothing and living upon nothing, better than the poor classes of Spain. Climate does one half, and temperament the rest. Give a Spaniard the shade in summer and the sun in winter, a little bread, garlic, oil, and *garbances,* an old brown cloak and a guitar and let the world roll on as it pleases. Talk of poverty! with him it has no disgrace. It sits upon him with a grandiose style, like his ragged cloak. He is a *hidalgo,* even when in rags.

The "sons of the Alhambra" are an eminent illustration of his practical philosophy. As the Moors imagined that the celestial pardaise hung over this favored spot, so I am inclined at times to fancy that a gleam of the golden age still lingers about this ragged community.

(The Alhambra)

Washington Irving

Sleepy Hollow

Irving at 22, crayon sketch by Vanderlyn.

Washington Irving

Diedrich Knickerbocker

THE LITTLE MAN IN BLACK.

SALMAGUNDI;

OR, THE

WHIM-WHAMS AND OPINIONS

OF

LAUNCELOT LANGSTAFF, ESQ.

AND OTHERS.

In hoc est hoax, cum quiz et jokesez,
Et smokem, toastem, roastem folksez,
Fee, faw, fum. *Psalmanazar.*
With baked, and broiled, and stewed, and toas
And fried, and boiled, and smoked, and roas
We treat the town.

VOL. II.

NEW-YORK:

PRINTED & PUBLISHED BY D. LONGWORTH,

At the Shakspeare-Gallery.

1808

*The first of these anonymous yellow-backed
pamphlets was published in January, 1807.*

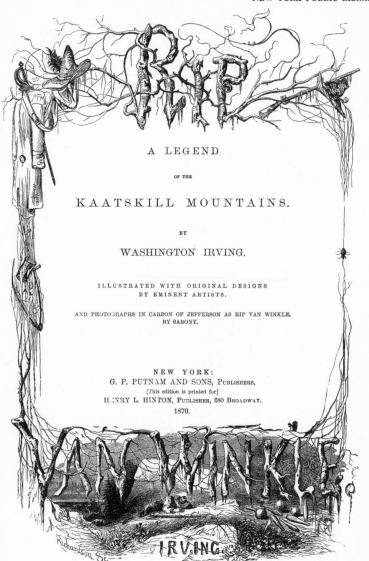

RIP

A LEGEND

OF THE

KAATSKILL MOUNTAINS.

BY

WASHINGTON IRVING.

ILLUSTRATED WITH ORIGINAL DESIGNS
BY EMINENT ARTISTS.

AND PHOTOGRAPHS IN CARBON OF JEFFERSON AS RIP VAN WINKLE,
BY SARONY.

NEW YORK:
G. P. PUTNAM AND SONS, Publishers.
[This edition is printed for]
HENRY L. HINTON, Publisher, 680 Broadway.
1870.

VAN WINKLE

IRVING

Richardson Sc.

JEFFERSON AS RIP VAN WINKLE

Irving and his literary friends at Sunnyside. Painting by Christian Schussele. Seated, l. to r.: William Gilmore Sims, Fitz-Green Halleck, William H. Prescott, Washington Irving, Ralph Waldo Emerson, James Fenimore Cooper and George

Bancroft. Standing l. to r.: Oliver Wendell Holmes, Nathaniel Hawthorne, Henry Wadsworth Longfellow, Nathaniel Parker Willis, James K. Paulding, William Cullen Bryant and John P. Kennedy.

The Headless Horseman from Legend of Sleepy Hollow, *lithograph by William J. Wilgus.*

Squire kept up old customs in kitchen as well as hall ; and the rolling-pin, struck upon the dresser by the cook, summoned the servants to carry in the meats.

Sir John Suckling
from Irving's Sketch Book
illustration by Ralph Caldecott.

*Photograph of Washington Irving
taken by Matthew Brady in the 1850s.*

As Others Saw Him

Before Washington Irving published his Sketch Book, *Old World critics held a low opinion of American writers. Here are some typical British judgments:*

"The Americans have no national literature, and no learned men. . . . There is no room amongst them, for such men as an Alfred, a Chaucer, a Spenser, a Bacon, a Newton, or a Locke; and, until their continent shall have once more been submerged in the waters of the ocean, there cannot possibly be such men in America."

—Anonymous English critic, 1818

"Where are their . . . Scotts, Campbells, Byrons, Moores, or Crabbes? . . . or their parallels to the hundred other names that have spread themselves over the world from our little island in the course of the last thirty years, and have blest or delighted mankind by their works? . . . There is no such parallel to be produced. . . . In the four quarters of the globe, who reads an American book?"

—*Sydney Smith*, 1820

"In America there is but one dialect. But to have this dialect likened, and even preferred, to the pure language of England, reminds us of the critical judges in the fable, who decided that the squeaking imitation of the pig was more natural than the real squeak of piggy himself."

—*Anonymous English critic*, 1821

["American] authors, without models of their own, are often too proud to form themselves upon those of other countries. . . . They have no foundation of their own to build on—nothing can come from nothing—and the consequence of their perverseness or blindness is, that all which they attempt of originality is an heterogeneous mass of unskilled plagiarism."

—*Anonymous English critic*, 1823

"What visions, what exalting ancestral recollections can the wand of poetry summon from the rude traffic of exiles with savages, from sectarian bickerings and Indian massacre, from the unhappy life of fugitives struggling with the difficulties of a strange and unpropitious land, or from the brutishness, squalidness, and ferocity of the wigwam?"

—*Anonymous English critic*, 1824

"America has hitherto had little or no originality in her literature, or, to speak more properly, she had done nothing but copy. . . . She had no religion, no manners, and, above all, no language, essentially her own. Peopled chiefly by the fanatic, the adventurer, and the criminal . . .—forced to live by the sweat of their brows—the farmer, the husbandman, and the woodsman, had little time, and less inclination, for literary pursuits."

—*Anonymous English critic*, 1825

Then Diedrich Knickerbocker, Ichabod Crane, and their companions crossed the Atlantic, and the Old World opinion was permanently changed. The criticisms of Irving which follow illustrate this change.

The meagre annals of this short-lived Dutch colony have afforded the groundwork for this amusing book, which is certainly the wittiest our press has ever produced. To examine it seriously in a historical point of view would be ridiculous; though the few important events of the period to which it relates are, we presume, recorded with accuracy as to their dates and consequences. . . .

The account of these honest Dutch governors has been made subservient to a lively flow of good-natured satire on the follies and blunders of the present day, and the perplexities they have caused.

—Anonymous American reviewer, c. 1810(?)
(Pierre M. Irving, *Life and Letters of Washington Irving,* I)

If it is true, as Sterne says, that a man draws a nail out of his coffin every time he laughs, after reading Irving's book [*Knickerbocker's History of New York*] your coffin will certainly fall to pieces.

—Anonymous correspondent, c. 1815
(Baltimore)

I beg you to accept my best thanks for the uncommon degree of entertainment which I have received from the most excellently jocose history of New York. I am sensible, that as a stranger to American parties and politics, I must lose much of the concealed satire of the piece, but I must own that looking at the simple and obvious meaning only, I have never read any thing so closely resembling the style of Dean [Jonathan] Swift, as the annals of Diedrich Knickerbocker [the *History of New York*]. I have been employed these few evenings in reading them aloud to Mrs. S. [Mrs. Scott], and two ladies who are our guests, and our sides have been absolutely sore with laughing.

[1813]

82

I . . . have glanced over *The Sketch Book*. It is positively beautiful. [1819]

—Sir Walter Scott, Scottish poet and novelist
(Pierre M. Irving, *Life and Letters of Washington Irving,* I)

It is painful to see a mind, as admirable for its exquisite perception of the beautiful, as it is for its quick sense of the ridiculous, wasting the riches of its fancy on an ungrateful theme, and its exuberant humour in a coarse caricature [in *Knickerbocker's History of New York*].

—Gulian C. Verplanck, American critic, 1818
(Discourses and Addresses on Subjects of American History, Arts, and Literature)

[In *The Sketch Book,* Irving] appears to have lost a little of the natural run of style for which his lighter writings were so remarkable. He has given up something of his direct, simple manner. . . . It is as if his mother-English had been sent abroad to be improved, and in attempting to become accomplished, had lost too many of her home qualities.

—Richard H. Dana, Sr., American critic, 1819
North American Review

You desire me to write to you my sentiments on reading *The Sketch Book,* No. II. . . . Everywhere I find in it the marks of a mind of the utmost elegance and refinement, a thing as you know that I was not exactly prepared to look for in an American. . . . There is wonderful sweetness in it.

—William Godwin, English philosopher, 1819
(Pierre M. Irving, *Life and Letters of Washington Irving,* I)

The great popularity of Mr. Irving's *Sketch Book* has excited considerable interest on the subject of American literature. Previously to the publication of that admirable miscellany, the literary compositions of our trans-Atlantic brethren had only provoked the spleen and contempt of the British critics . . ., the *Edinburgh* attributing it [American inferiority] to their [the Americans'] mechanical and mercantile habits and avocations; while the *Quarterly* ascribed it to the stupidity which they, in common with all nations who are in the least hostile to our virtuous ministers [statesmen] . . ., must necessarily possess. Since the appearance of the *Sketch Book,* the tone of our haughty reviewers is somewhat altered.

—Anonymous English critic, 1820
*(The London Magazine and Monthly Critical
and Dramatic Review)*

We require such works as the *Rambler* [by Dr. Samuel Johnson] and books of that description, moral and learned and argumentative writers. . . .

Such works are rare in our American literature and we all feel the deficiency. . . . Books of an ephemeral nature like the *Sketch-Book* will not remedy the evil. Although we feel the beauty of his [Irving's] description, although we love the picturesque glitter of a summer morning's landscape as much as any yet we would willingly exchange the transient pleasure for those of active and salutary effect whose tendency is to instruct and improve rather than to entertain.

[1820, *Notebooks*]

Our economical citizens have been quite dead to *Bracebridge Hall,* since its price was known, and I have neither read it, nor seen a single individual who has read it. The extracts which I have met with, have disappointed me much, as he has left his fine *Sketch Book* style, for the deplorable Dutch wit of *Knickerbocker,* which to me is very tedious.

[1822, *Letters*]

Irving is a word-catcher.

[1828, *Journals*]

Ah, my country! In thee is the reasonable hope of mankind not fulfilled. It should be that when all feudal straps and bandages were taken off an unfolding of the Titans had followed. . . . But the utmost thou hast yet produced, is a puny love of beauty in Allston, in Greenough; in Bryant; in Everett; in Channing; in Irving; an imitative love of grace.

[1838, *Journals*]

84

Irving, Bryant, Greenough, Everett, Channing, even Webster . . . all lack nerve and dagger.

[1839, *Journals*]

All the notable Americans, except Webster, as I have said before, are female minds; Channing, Irving, Everett, Greenough, Allston, etc.

[1846, *Journals*]

—Ralph Waldo Emerson, American essayist, 1820-1846

The whole book [*Knickerbocker's History of New York*] is *ajeu-d'esprit,* and perhaps its only fault is that no *jeu-d'esprit* ought to be quite so long as to fill two closely-printed volumes.

—J. G. Lockhart, Scottish critic, and biographer, 1820
(*Blackwood's Magazine*)

His Crayon [Irving's *Sketch Book*]—I know it by heart, at least there is not a passage that I cannot refer to immediately.

[Byron] had been delighted with *Knickerbocker's History of New York,* which he seemed to prefer of all Irving's works; and though he thought Irving's style became afterward "rather florid," he commended it very highly. . . . Byron [said] that his esteem for Irving was common to all his countrymen.

—Lord Byron, English poet, 1820–1822
(in Pierre M. Irving, *Life and Letters of Washington
Irving,* II; and in Ernest J. Lovell, Jr., *His
Very Self and Voice*)

He [Lord Byron] rose from his couch when I entered, and, pressing my hand warmly, said, "Have you brought *The Sketch Book?*" I handed it to him; when, seizing it with enthusiasm, he turned to "The Broken Heart."

"That," said he, "is one of the finest things ever written on earth; and I want to hear an American read it. But stay! Do you know Irving?" I replied that I had never seen him. "God bless him!" exclaimed Byron: "he is a genius; and he has something better than genius—a heart. I wish I could see him; but

I fear I never shall. Well, read 'The Broken Heart,'—yes, 'The Broken Heart.' What a word!"

In closing the first paragraph, I said, "Shall I confess it? I believe in broken hearts."

"Yes," exclaimed Byron, "and so do I, and so does everybody but philosophers and fools." While I was reading one of the most touching portions of that mournful piece, I observed that Byron wept. He turned his eyes upon me, and said, "You see me weep, sir. Irving himself never wrote that story without weeping; nor can I hear it without tears. I have not wept much in this world, for trouble never brings tears to my eyes; but I always have tears for 'The Broken Heart.' . . . Sir, how many such men as Washington Irving are there in America?"

—Anonymous American traveler, 1824
("Byron" in Allibone's Dictionary of Authors, I)

This [Irving's *Sketch Book*] is one of the best samples which we have yet seen of American literature; for though it is, as indeed it professes to be, of a light and unpretending character, it is good of its kind; full of imagination, and embellished with a delicacy of feeling, and a refinement of taste, that do not often belong to our transatlantic descendants.

—Anonymous English critic, 1821
(Quarterly Review)

What person, unless he possessed some previous knowledge of the fact, could tell, upon reading the greater and the better part of Mr. Irving's works, that he was not an Englishman? It is . . . notorious that his writings have had a certain beneficial effect upon the literature of the day in both nations [England and America]. —Anonymous English critic, 1822

(British Magazine)

Are you not pleased with *Bracebridge Hall*? He is a witty amiable sort of person *Mr.* Irving; but oh he wants fire, and he is *far too happy* for me.

—Jane Welsh (later Mrs. Thomas Carlyle), Scottish critic, 1822

(Charles R. Sanders, ed., Collected Letters of Thomas
and Jane Welsh Carlyle)

I perfectly agree with your view of Washington [Irving]—
a smooth polished clever amiable man—excellent for an acquaintance—but for a bosom-friend—*no!*

—Thomas Carlyle, Scottish essayist and historian, 1822
(Charles R. Sanders, ed., *Collected Letters of Thomas
and Jane Welsh Carlyle*)

The great charm and peculiarity of his work consists now,
as on former occasions, in the singular sweetness of the composition, and the mildness of the sentiments,—sicklied over
perhaps a little, now and then, with that cloying heaviness into
which unvaried sweetness is so apt to subside. The rhythm and
melody of the sentences is certainly excessive; as it not only
gives an air of mannerism, but raises too strong an impression of the labour that must have been bestowed, and the im-
portance which must have been attached to that which is, after
all, but a secondary attribute to good writing. It is very ill-na-
tured in us, however, to object to what has given us so much
pleasure; for we happen to be very intense and sensitive admirers of those soft harmonies of studied speech in which this
author is apt to indulge himself.

—Lord Jeffrey, Scottish critic, 1822
(Edinburgh Review)

We confess that we regard Mr. Washington Irving with a very
evil eye. We owe him a grudge, firstly for being an American,
and presuming to write in the very best and purest style of
the English language; secondly, that he has dared to rival our
standard writers, in wit, humour, pathos, and characteristic
description; thirdly, lastly and worstly, that not content to
remain in his own country . . . he has come over here, reaped
a rich harvest . . . and contrived to have his name inserted in
the scroll of fame as the first essayist of America, and in the
very foremost rank of those of Britain.

—Anonymous English critic, 1823
(Literary Museum)

Previously to the arrival of Geoffrey Crayon [Washington
Irving], we had been accustomed to regard the productions of

our Trans-Atlantic brethren with a supercilious eye; but from the moment that the writings of Irving became popular, it has been the fashion to admire and extol American literature.

—Anonymous English critic, 1823
(Monthly Literary Register)

I take the opportunity . . . to tell you, [Irving], that your book [*Tales of a Traveller*] is delightful. I never can answer for what the public will like, but if they do not devour this with their best appetite, then is good writing, good fun, good sense, and all other goods of authorship thrown away upon them.

I had to listen to Lord Lansdowne the other evening reading over whole pages of Buckthorne [from *Tales of a Traveller*] which I already knew by heart, but which he seemed so pleased with that it would have been a sin to stop him. Luttrell also has been warm in your praises, and altogether your muse, I think, treads upon velvet.

—Thomas Moore, Irish poet, 1824
(Pierre M. Irving, *Life and Letters of Washington Irving,* II)

[Washington Irving] was never remarkable for originality of genius, richness of invention, or vivacity of fancy. No man in the republic of letters has been more overrated than Mr. Washington Irving. With very moderate powers of *description,* he has been *puffed* to an artificial magnitude, which he cannot realize by his productions. Take away his *Dutchman with his pipe; his old mansion with his Ghosts, his Uncle Trim, and his Aunt Tabitha*—and perhaps a clown of an *Old Bachelor,* and Mr. Irving is like the lion with his claws drawn out. . . . GHOST STORIES! ! . . .

But he who writes for the sole purpose of obtaining money, is entitled to no praise, because he selects topics that will excite the popular passions. . . . This Mr. Irving has done. He knew Ghost merchandise would sell to the best advantage. . . .

It is suggested that Mr. Washington Irving's new work would sell more rapidly if the Booksellers would alter the Title, and call it "STORIES FOR CHILDREN" by *a Baby Six Feet High,* instead of *Tales of a Traveller.*

—Anonymous American critic, 1824

(New York Mirror)

Geoffrey's [Irving's] fame was occasioned by the fact of his being a *prodigy;* . . . up to the time of Geoffrey, there were no Belles Lettres in America, no native *litterateurs,* and he shot up at once with true American growth, a triumphant proof of what had so long been doubted and denied, namely, that the sentimental plant may flourish even on that republican soil. . . . The surprise that a Chinese should express himself in pure English, could not have been greater than that such a production should come from such a quarter. . . .

[But Irving presented] nothing that can excite controversy, nothing that can occasion dissatisfaction; all, pensive, gentlemanly, and subdued; . . . prevailing errors in morals and legislation carefully upheld, or, at best, left unnoticed . . . a little pathos, a little sentiment, to excite tears as a pleasurable emotion for those who see them on no other occasion.

—Anonymous English critic, 1824

(Westminster Review)

Mr. Irving is by birth an American, and has, as it were, *skimmed the cream,* and taken off patterns with great skill and cleverness, from our best known and happiest writers, so that their thoughts and almost their reputation are indirectly transferred to his page. . . .

Mr. Irving's writings [*The Sketch Book,* and *Bracebridge Hall*] are literary *anachronisms.* He comes to England for the first time; and being on the spot, fancies himself in the midst of those characters and manners which he had read of in the *Spectator* and other approved authors, and which were the only idea he had hitherto formed of the parent country. Instead of looking round to see what *we are,* he sets to work to describe us as *we were*—at second hand. . . .

Instead of tracing the changes that have taken place in society since Addison or Fielding wrote, he transcribes their accounts in a different hand-writing, and thus keeps us stationary, at least in our most attractive and praise-worthy qualities of simplicity, honesty, modesty, hospitality, and good-nature.

This is a very flattering mode of turning fiction into history, or history into fiction; and we should scarcely know ourselves again in the softened and altered likeness, but that it bears the date of 1820, and issues from the press in Albemarle-street. This is one way of complimenting our national and Tory prejudices; and coupled with literal or exaggerated portraits of *Yankee* peculiarities, could hardly fail to please.

—William Hazlitt, English critic, 1825
(The Spirit of the Age)

The Sketch-Book is a timid, beautiful work; with some childish pathos in it; some rich, pure, bold poetry: a little squeamish, puling, lady-like sentimentality; some courageous writing, some wit, and a world of humour, so happy, so natural, so altogether unlike that of any other man, dead or alive, that we would rather have been the writer of it, fifty times over, than of every thing else that he has ever written.

The touches of poetry are everywhere; but never where we would look for them. Irving has no passion; he fails utterly in true pathos,—cannot speak as if he were carried away by any thing. He is always thoughtful; and, save when he tries to be fine or sentimental, always natural. The "dusty splendour" of Westminster Abbey, the "ship staggering" over the precipices of the ocean, the shark "darting, like spectre, through the waters,"—all these things are poetry, such poetry as never was, never will be, surpassed.   —John Neal, English critic, 1825
(Blackwood's Magazine)

My impression [of Irving's *Conquest of Granada*] is that, with much elegance, there is mixed a good deal of affectation— I must add, of feebleness. He is not the man to paint tumultuous war.   —J. G. Lockhart, Scottish critic and biographer, 1827
(Samuel Smiles, *A Publisher and His Friends*)

[Washington Irving's] style is undoubtedly one of the most finished and agreeable forms in which the English language has ever been presented. . . . Its peculiar characteristic is a continual and sustained elegance.

Salmagundi and the *History of New York* . . . exhibit the talent of the author, in the full perfection of its power. . . .

[In *Salmagundi*] Mr. Irving appears to have no other object in view, but that of making a sprightly book and laughing at everything laughable. . . .

Salmagundi was pretty soon followed by the *History of New York*. This we consider . . . [the work] which exhibits most distinctly the stamp of real inventive power, the true test . . . of genius. . . The graphic distinctness, with which the three Dutch governors, whom nobody ever heard of before, are made to pass before us . . . is quite admirable; and the political satire is conveyed with great effect. . . .

At length he brought out the *Sketch Book*. . . . The characteristics of the *Sketch Book* are essentially the same with those of the preceding works; but, with somewhat more polish and elegance, it has somewhat less vivacity, freshness, and power. . . . The Crayons and Bracebridges . . . are Sketches indeed, and in water colors, compared with the living roaring group of Cockloft Hall [in *Salmagundi*]; and although we find occasional returns of the author's best manner in "The Stout Gentleman," "Rip Van Winkle," "Sleepy Hollow," "The Moneydiggers," and so forth, the right material employed in these pieces is not, as before, the staple of the work, but a passing refreshment.

—Alexander H. Everett, American critic, 1829
(North American Review)

The want of originality in American literature is, we think, likely long to continue. . . . At least it will continue until a dozen or two minds such as the authors of *Knickerbocker* [Washington Irving] and the *Pioneers* [James Fenimore Cooper], shall shed the radiance of their genius over the infant literature of America.

—Anonymous English critic, 1831
(Athenaeum)

Washington Irving has been staying some weeks in my house. . . . An intimate acquaintance with him, has satisfied me, that I was mistaken in supposing, that his literary occupation had given his mind a turn unfavourable to practical business pursuits. . . . So far from it, I have been both disappointed, and pleased, to find in him, not only great capacity, but an active and untiring disposition for the prompt, and successful discharge of business.

—Martin Van Buren, American Statesman and President, 1831
   (*Correspondence of Andrew Jackson,* ed. John S. Bassett, IV)

The *Tales of the Alhambra* are brilliant and striking, told with the most delightful grace of language, and addressed to the imagination of all classes. . . . They are evidently no inventions, but transcripts. His scenes stretch away before you; his people move, look, and walk with an individuality and a force only to be produced by the hand of a master. . . . [They are] worthy of the best parts of the *Sketch Book*.

—Anonymous American critic, 1832
[New York *Mirror*]

Washington Irving, when he came to this country, and gave the world, under the name of the *Sketch-Book,* his first cis-atlantic [this side of the Atlantic] productions, did judiciously in selecting the pseudonym of Geoffrey Crayon for his writings and paintings. They are works of art. . . . He does not teach; he does not narrate; he does not celebrate; he catches situations; he has an eye for effects, moral and picturesque; and he employs and works them into his pictures . . . and lends them all the advantages to be derived from nice [accurate] drawing, accurate perspective, tasteful disposition, and, above all, a rich and mellow colouring which spreads a glow over his subjects.

—Anonymous English critic, 1832
   (*Westminster Review*)

[Irving's *A Tour on the Prairies*] is a sort of sentimental journey, a romantic excursion. . . . We are proud of Mr. Irving's sketches of English life, proud of the gorgeous canvas upon

92

which he has gathered in so much of the glowing imagery of Moorish times. . . . But we glow with rapture as we see him coming back, laden with the poetical treasures of the primitive wilderness, rich with spoil from the uninhabited desert [the American West]. We thank him for turning these poor barbarous *steppes* into classical land.

—Edward Everett, American critic, 1835
(North American Review)

The *Crayon Miscellany* [by Washington Irving] . . . is the tribute of genius to its kindred spirits, and it breathes a sanctifying influence over the graves of the departed. The kindly feelings of Irving are beautifully developed in his description of the innocent pursuits and cheerful conversation of Sir Walter Scott, while they give a melancholy interest to the early misfortunes of Byron. . . . In nothing that he has ever written, has his peculiar faculty of imparting to all he touches the coloring of his genius, been more fully displayed than in this work.

[1835, *Southern Literary Messenger*]

Irving is much overrated, and a nice [fine] distinction might be drawn between his just and his surreptitious and adventitious reputation—between what is due to the pioneer solely, and what to the writer.

The merit, too, of his tame propriety and faultlessness of style should be candidly weighed. . . . A bold . . . investigation of Irving's claims would strike home, take my word for it.

[1838, *Letter*]

You know Irving heads the school of the *quietists*.

[1839, *Letter*]

The Essays of Hawthorne have much of the character of Irving, with more of originality, and less of finish; while, compared with the *Spectator,* they have a vast superiority at all points. The *Spectator,* Mr. Irving, and Mr. Hawthorne have in common that tranquil and subdued manner which we have chosen to denominate *repose;* but, in the case of the two former [Irving and the *Spectator*], this repose is attained rather by the absence of novel combinations, or of originality, than otherwise, and consists chiefly in the calm, quiet, unostentatious expression of commonplace thoughts, in an unambitious, unadulterated Saxon. In them, by strong effort, we are made to conceive the absence of all. [1842, *Graham's Magazine*]

We have very few American tales of real merit—we may say, indeed, none, with the exception of *The Tales of a Traveller* of Washington Irving, and these *Twice-Told Tales* of Mr. Hawthorne. [1842, *Graham's Magazine*]

Of skillfully-constructed tales—I speak now without reference to other points, some of them more important than construction—there are very few American specimens. . . . *The Tales of a Traveller,* by Irving, are graceful and impressive narratives—"The Young Italian" is especially good—but there is not one of the series which can be commended as a whole. In many of them the interest is subdivided and frittered away, and their conclusions are insufficiently *climactic.*

—Edgar Allan Poe, American poet and critic, 1835-1847
[1847, *Godey's Lady's Book*]

Not such works as, in her after-dinner doze,
Dame IRVING ravels from her worn-out hose;
Which we the town for bran-new worsted buy
And quote as extra-fine, yet know not why. . . .

This, I have no doubt, will be the first time that Mr. IRVING has heard the truth since he rose to eminence. . . . Mr. IRVING's distinguished excellence, then, is *good taste;* a merit in composition not the commonest in this day. . . . As the author of the *Sketch Book* began, so he continues, and so he will end . . . and those who really admire this excellent writer (and they are not those who flatter him most,) these, I say, must regret to see him *dawdling* in such books as the *Crayon Miscellany.*

—Laughton Osborn, American poet, 1838
(The Vision of Rubeta)

There is no man in the World who could have given me the heartfelt pleasure you have, by your kind note of the Thirteenth of last Month. There is no living writer, and there are very few among the dead, whose approbation I should feel so proud to earn. And with everything you have written, upon my shelves, and in my thoughts, and in my heart of hearts, I may honestly and truly say so. If you could know how earnestly I write this, you would be glad to read it—as I hope you will be, faintly guessing at the warmth of the hand I autographically hold out to you, over the broad Atlantic.

I wish I could find in your welcome letter, some hint of an intention to visit England. . . . I should love to go with you—as I have gone, God knows how often—into Little Britain, and Eastcheap, and Green Arbour Court, and Westminster Abbey. I should like to travel with you, outside the last of the coaches, down to Bracebridge Hall. . . . *Diedrich Knickerbocker* I have worn to death in my pocket—and yet I should shew you his mutilated carcass—with a joy past all expression.

I have been so accustomed to associate you with my pleasantest and happiest thoughts, and with my leisure hours, that I rush at once into full confidence with you. . . . I hope to have many letters from you, and to exchange a frequent correspondence.

—Charles Dickens, English novelist, 1841
(Madeline House and Graham Storey, ed.,
Letters of Charles Dicken, II)

I have never had any quarrel with Mr. Irving, and give him full credit as a writer. Still, I believe him to be below the ordinary level, in moral qualities, instead of being above them, as he is cried up to be. I believe the same to have been the case with Scott, whom I know for a double-dealer. . . . Bryant is worth forty Irvings, in every point of view, but he runs a little into the seemly school.

—James Fenimore Cooper, American novelist, 1842
*(Passages from the Correspondence and Other Papers of
Rufus W. Griswold)*

95

I have found [Washington Irving] a most delightful companion. He is cheerful, gay, talkative, and appears to be no longer subject to those moody fits which formerly obscured his fine intellect at times, as the dark clouds flit across the face of the brightest summer's day.   [1833, *Dairy*]

I have passed a few hours delightfully in reading Washington Irving's "Tour on the Prairies." It is of the very best kind of light reading. Killing buffaloes, hunting wild horses, sleeping every night on the ground for a whole month . . . are events of ordinary interest to the settlers in the great west, but they are matters of thrilling interest to citizens who read of them in their green slippers seated before a shining grate. [1835, *Diary*]

Dickens was at the levee [reception given by President Tyler], and Washington Irving, and as far as I could judge Irving out-bozzed Boz [Dickens]. He collected a crowd around him; the men pressed on to shake his hand, and the women to touch the hem of his garment. Somebody told me that they saw a woman put on his hat, in order—as she told her companions—that she might have it to say that she had worn Washington Irving's hat. All this was "fun to them" . . . but "death to" poor Irving, who has no relish for this sort of glorification, and less tact than any man living to get along with it decently.   [1842, *Diary*]
>   —Philip Hone, American politician and philanthropist,
>   1833–1842

What! Irving? thrice welcome, warm heart and fine brain,
You bring back the happiest spirit from Spain,
And the gravest sweet humor, that ever were there
Since Cervantes met death in his gentle despair. . . .
To a true poet-heart add the fun of Dick Steele,
Throw in all of Addison, *minus* the chill,
With the whole of that partnership's stock and good will,
Mix well, and while stirring, hum o'er, as a spell,
The fine *old* English Gentleman, simmer it well . . .
And you'll find a choice nature, not wholly deserving
A name either English or Yankee—just Irving.
>   [1848, *A Fable for Critics*]

[Washington] Irving . . . after humorously satirizing the poverty of our annals in his *Knickerbocker,* forced to feel the pensive beauty of what is ancient by the painful absence of it, first tried to create an artificial antiquity as a substitute, and then sought in the Old World a kindlier atmosphere and themes more sympathetic with the dainty and carefully shaded phrase he loved. He first taught us the everliving charm of style, most invaluable and most difficult of lessons. Almost wholly English, he is yet our earliest classic.   [1887, *Literary Criticism*]

—James Russell Lowell, American poet and essayist,
1848–1887

Candor, good judgment that knows no bias, the felicity of selection, these are yours, [dear Irving], in common with the best historians. But, in addition, you have the peculiarity of writing from the heart, enchaining sympathy as well as commanding confidence; the happy magic that makes scenes, events, and personal anecdotes present themselves to you at your bidding, and fall into their natural places, and take color and warmth, from your own nature. The style, too, is masterly, clear, easy, and graceful; picturesque without mannerism, and ornamented without losing simplicity.

—George Bancroft, American historian, 1855
(Pierre M. Irving, *Life and Letters of Washington Irving,* IV)

I have been gladdened by the sight of the second volume of your great work [Irving's *Life of Washington*]. . . . You have done with Washington just as I thought you would, and, instead of a cold, marble statue of a demigod, you have made him a being of flesh and blood, like ourselves—one with whom we can have sympathy.

—William H. Prescott, American historian, 1856
(Pierre M. Irving, *Life and Letters of Washington Irving,* IV)

Every reader has his first book; I mean to say, one book among all others which in early youth first fascinates his imagination, and at once excites and satisfies the desires of his mind. To me, this first book was *The Sketch Book* of Washington Irving. I was a school-boy when it was published, and read each succeeding number with ever increasing wonder and delight, spell-bound by its pleasant humor, its melancholy tenderness, its atmosphere of revery—nay, even by its gray-brown covers, the shaded letters of its titles, and the fair clean type.

—Henry Wadsworth Longfellow, American poet, 1859
(Proceedings of the Massachusetts Historical Society)

[Washington Irving] was the first ambassador whom the New World of Letters sent to the Old. He was born almost with the republic; the *pater patriae* [father of his country] had laid his hand on the child's head. He bore Washington's name: he came amongst us bringing the kindest sympathy, the most artless, smiling good-will. His new country . . . could send us, as he showed in his own person, a gentleman, who, though himself born in no very high sphere, was most finished, polished, easy, witty, quiet; and, socially, the equal of the most refined Europeans.

—William Makepeace Thackeray, English novelist, 1860
(Roundabout Papers)

[Irving's] *Salmagundi* is the literary parent not only of the *Sketch Book,* but of all the intermediate and subsequent productions of Irving. . . . There is, for instance . . . a chapter . . . which anticipates the humor of *Knickerbocker;* there are traits of tenderness and pathos suggestive of the plaintive sentiment of the *Sketch Book;* and the kindly humors of the Cockloft mansion are an American Bracebridge Hall.

—Evert A. Duyckinck, American critic, 1860
(Washington Irving, *Salmagundi,* Duyckinck, ed.)

His was not a nature to pry for faults, or disabuse the world of good-natured mistakes; he looked for virtue, love, and truth among men, and thanked God that he found them in such large measure. If there are touches of satire in his writings, he is the best-natured and most amiable of satirists—amiable beyond Horace; and in his irony—for there is a vein of playful irony running through many of his works—there is no tinge of bitterness.

—William Cullen Bryant, American poet, 1860
(Washington Irving, A Discourse on His Life, Character and Genius)

It is the fashion with some readers to depreciate Washington Irving's writings as of too flimsy and voluble a texture. But we are persuaded that, as in beauty of style they can never become obsolete so long as the English classics are read, so in their literary worth, as throwing much light upon the growth of a colonial literature, they must rise rather than fall in the estimation of scholars.

—Anonymous English critic, 1863
(Spectator)

[In his boyhood, Washington Irving] procured a number of the old English authors, and read with delight the poems of Chaucer and Spenser. The gay humor of the one, and the rich imagination of the other, served to cultivate the faculties, from whose combination, in his own works, Irving was destined to derive so much fame.

—William Watson Waldron, American biographer, 1867
(Washington Irving and Contemporaries)

Mr. Irving was one of the not very numerous class of writers who become rich by authorship; and, whatever may be thought of his lack of business capacity otherwise, certain it is that his transactions with his several publishers indicate no such deficiency.

From most of his works he shrewdly managed to reap a double harvest, English and American; selling at once his copyrights to his English publishers, and leasing them to his publishers at home. Thus we have the following exhibit . . ..

AMOUNTS REALIZED FROM THE SALE OF
COPYRIGHTS IN ENGLAND

Sketch-Book, 467 10s., or about	$2,338	00
Bracebridge Hall	5,250	00
Tales of a Traveller	7,875	00
Life of Columbus	15,750	00
Companions of Columbus	2,625	00
Conquest of Granada	10,500	00
Tour on the Prairies	2,000	00
Abbotsford and Newstead	2,000	00
Legends of Spain	500	00
Alhambra	5,250	00
Astoria	2,500	00
Bonneville's, Adventures	4,500	00
Amount	$61,088	00

AMOUNTS REALIZED IN THE UNITED STATES FOR
LEASES OF COPYRIGHTS

Columbus	$3,000	00
Abridgment of Columbus	6,000	00
Conquest of Granada	4,750	00
Companions of Columbus	1,500	00
Alhambra	3,000	00
Tour on the Prairies	2,400	00
Abbotsford and Newstead	2,100	00
Legends of the Conquest of Spain	1,500	00
Astoria	4,000	00
Bonneville's Adventures	3,000	00
Knickerbocker, Sketch-Book, Bracebridge Hall, and Tales	4,200	00
Receipts for the last four works previous to 1828	19,500	00
Further lease of these four and other works	8,050	00
Amount for leases of copyright	$63,000	00

After the arrangement with Mr. Putnam for the uniform

edition of his works, Mr. Irving, up to the time of his decease, received from his publisher, (besides the stereotype and steel plates, valued at $17,000) $88,143 00

Add the foregoing amount from leases	63,000 00
Add also the foregoing amount from English copyrights	61,088 00
Amount received in his life-time	$212,231 00
Add the amount received in four years after his death	34,237 00
Whole amount from his writing up to 1864	$256,468 00

Hence it is certain that Irving's picture of "Poor Devil Author" was but very slightly applicable to himself.

—Charles Adams, American biographer, 1870
(Memoir of Washington Irving)

Aside from the inscrutable element in great men . . . , there are certain determinable factors which give distinctness to their lives and works. In Irving these are four: (1) extraordinary sensibility to impressions from the material world; (2) a remarkable faculty of form; (3) a deficiency of analytic power; and (4) a cosmopolitan life.

His sensibility to the beauties of nature is discernible in his earliest letters; for even in these he paints the scenery of the noble Hudson and the incidents of his first travels with accuracy of detail, and warmth of color. It is not less evident in his early caricatures of society, which, while often fanciful, are sometimes vividly descriptive. . . .

His characters are such as have actually lived and moved among men, rather than ideals elaborated by the creative imagination out of the plastic elements of life. They have been seen in his travels, or have been built up by the fancy, which patches rather than creates, out of the fragmentary views furnished by old traditions or curious chronicles. . . .

His lack of analytic power explains the absence of conscious moral purpose in his works. His writings are spiritually healthful, but not by intention. They happen to be so because of his intrinsic nobility. . . . Failing . . . to connect social factors and social wrongs, he never commended a creed, or advocated a theory. By no means indifferent to the ills of humanity, he left the race to solve its own problems without his advice. For this silence he has been blamed, and shares, in the estimation of the strong-minded, in the character of his "golden-hearted man," whom Carlyle reproachfully calls "the pretty-story-telling Walter Scott."

—David J. Hill, American biographer, 1879
(Washington Irving)

His predominant traits were humor and sentiment; his temperament was gay with a dash of melancholy; his inner life and his mental operations were the reverse of complex, and his literary method is simple. He *felt* his subject, and he expressed his conception . . . by almost imperceptible touches and shadings here and there. . . .

The analysis of a nature so simple and a character so transparent as Irving, who lived in the sunlight and had no envelope of mystery, has not the fascination that attaches to Hawthorne. . . .

His face was set towards the past, not towards the future. He never caught the restlessness of this century [the nineteenth], nor the prophetic light that shone in the faces of Coleridge, Shelley, and Keats. . . . He . . . belonged rather to the age of Addison than to that of Macaulay. And his placid, retrospective, optimistic strain pleased a public that were excited and harrowed by the mocking and lamenting of Lord Byron.

—Charles Dudley Warner, American biographer, 1881
(Washington Irving)

He is the first of the American humorists, as he is almost the first of the American writers; yet, belonging to the New World, there is a quaint Old World flavor about him.

He is refreshingly deliberate; never in a hurry.

Like BYRON'S "gentleman," he "never perspires."

He takes his time and tells you his story in his own way.

102

The most delightful of gossips, the most ingratiating of "Roundabouts." . . .

He knows how to be solid, to choose his words, to look all round his thoughts, to have thoughts that will bear looking at.

His wit is never forced; he is seldom on the broad grin.

In him, indeed, are germs of an American humor since run to seed in buffoonery; but he is never outrageous—always within delicate bounds.

His fun never goes mad, but is in excellent subordination to his narrative or discourse.

His wit plays about his subject like summer lightning. His laugh, or more often his grave smile, rises naturally, and is never affected; he is never strained or flashing, but often full of a deep and pathetic purpose; and his jokes, when they come, seem woven into the very texture of his style, instead of sticking up outside like a cocked hat!

We have seldom the rollicking fun of DICKENS, but often a touch of his tenderness.

It is the satire of SWIFT, without his sour coarseness.

The grace of STERNE, without his sham sentiment.

The delicate flavor of CHARLES LAMB, without, however, the sly but severe bite of LAMB's satire. . . .

If I ask what is the secret of IRVING's power, I find it to lie in a certain quiet absorption and concentration.

He identifies himself absolutely with whatever he is about; a man is always attractive and interesting if he will do that. As a consequence, we get a photographic minuteness of detail, the graphic points always being instinctively selected for the high lights.

—H. R. Haweis, English critic, 1881
(American Humorists)

The life of Washington Irving was one of the brightest ever led by an author. He discovered his genius at an early age; was graciously welcomed by his countrymen; answered the literary condition of the period when he appeared; won easily, and as easily kept, a distinguished place in the republic of letters; was generously rewarded for his work; charmed his contemporaries by his amiability and modesty; lived long, wisely, happily, and died at a ripe old age, in the fullness of his powers and his fame.

—Richard Henry Stoddard, American biographer, 1883
(The Works of Washington Irving)

[Washington] Irving's *Columbus* seemed to me a very good book. . . . [But] not to speak of errors and omissions which no historian could avoid so long as certain documents were yet unknown, Irving's book lacks the underlaying, so to speak, which is now deemed essential to every important historical composition; that is, it must not be narrative only, but also, and especially, discussive and critical.

Irving, then, may and does answer perfectly the purpose of the general reader—and he never purposed to himself any other aim; yet, above that class of readers who only seek to while away their spare time or acquire common notions, there exist historical students, exacting, robust and eager to know the why and wherefore of events.

—Henry Harrisse, American historian, c. 1884 (?)
(Manuscript Autobiography, New York Public Library)

I confess I heard not without a secret pleasure that the relic-hunters so chip and hammer the stone that marks Irving's grave as to make its frequent renewal necessary. It did not seem to me a grievous wrong . . . but rather a testimony to the loveableness of Irving's character, and an evidence of the wide extent of his fame, that, from filling the circle of the educated . . . has now come to include that lower stratum of our common humanity which has only instinctive and, so to speak, mechanical ways of expressing its feelings. . . .

[A] grudge . . . existed against him [Irving] in the minds of the descendants of the early Dutch settlers, on account of his "History of New York." . . . [They complained] that Irving had made New York ridiculous. . . . I could not sympathize. . . . As I looked at the matter, I thought New Yorkers ought to be much obliged to Irving for having built up so lively a structure on the flat marshland of their early history. And why should not New York have a fanciful early history as well as Rome or England? We read the stories of the Greek cities as if we believed them. . . . Is it not likely that the stories of Menelaus and Helen, of the wooden horse, and of sulking Achilles, were as disagreeable to old Greek and Trojan families as the fables of Van Twiller and Stuyvesant were to the old New Yorkers? . . .

If the parlor was somewhat bare [at Tarrytown], Mr. Irving's study was hardly more attractive. It was a small room, to the right on entering, with windows looking to the south and east; that facing the east was framed in . . . ivy . . . In the middle of the room was the plain table, always in a state of healthy disorder, at which Irving wrote, and at the north end was an alcove filled with books. . . .

This absence of picturesque . . . surroundings . . . was quickly forgotten, however, by all who met him [Irving], in the charms of his manners, and in the pleasure of listening to his talk. . . . He had at fifty-seven . . . the unconscious animal spirits of a boy. He could make himself at home with anybody, and put a child, or even a bore, at his ease. . . . Easy and natural as were Mr. Irving's manners, there was a strong individuality behind them; they are reflected in his books, whose limpid style seems so easy to imitate, and yet is beyond the reach of effort.

—Clarence Cook, American journalist, 1887
("A Glimpse of Washington Irving at Home,"
Century Magazine)

It is not difficult to infer the source of his many-hued characters and the odd situations in which he places some of them; his sketches doubtless are the result of his early habits of close observation, as well as fondness for adventure and travel. He said, indeed, that he was always fond of visiting strange characters and scenes, and it has been his fortune to have his roving passion gratified. . . .

In the picturesque words of a scholarly writer of our day (Dr. J. M. Taylor): ". . . Irving's genius was what, in the old English phrase, would have been called sauntering; it cast the glamour of idleness over our sharp, positive, and busy American life. Rip Van Winkle, the indolent and kindly vagabond, asserts the charm of day-dream and loitering against all the engrossing hurry of lucrative activity. . . . The vagabond of the Hudson is an unwasting figure of the imagination, the earliest, constant, gentlest satirist of American life."

—Frederick Saunders, American biographer, 1894
(Character Studies)

I did not perceive then [in my youth] that Irving's charm came largely from Cervantes and the other Spanish humorists . . . and that he had formed himself upon them almost as much as upon Goldsmith. . . . Afterward I came to see it, and at the same time to see what was Irving's own in Irving; to feel his native, if somewhat attenuated humor, and his original, if somewhat too studied grace. But as yet there was no critical question with me. I gave my heart simply and passionately to the author who made the scenes of that most pathetic history [*The Conquest of Granada*] live in my sympathy.

—William Dean Howells, American novelist, 1895
(My Literary Passions)

One thing . . . is pretty clear: the man had no message. From beginning to end he was animated by no profound sense of the mystery of existence. Neither the solemn eternities which stir philosophers and theologians, nor the actual lessons as distinguished from the superficial circumstances of human experience, ever much engaged his thought. Delicate, refined, romantic sentiment he set forth in delicate, refined classic style. One may wonder whether he had much to say; one can never question that he wrote beautifully.

—Barrett Wendell, American critic, 1901
(A Literary History of America)

He has had more praise for his style than for anything else; indeed, it has been commonly suggested that there is little else to praise him for. . . .

As far as the external features of his style are concerned, he has had praise enough, and more than enough. Clearness, ease, a certain Gallic grace it has; the ink flows readily, the thing says itself without crabbedness or constraint. On the other hand this ready writer is often conventional; a set phrase contents him, why should he labor to escape the usual formula? . . . The subtle artfulness of [Robert Louis] Stevenson is beyond him; but he has a rarer quality—that subtler artlessness which has belonged in some measure to all the greater writers of sentiment. . . .

It seems idle to say of such a man that because he does not concern himself with "the mystery of existence," and "the solemn eternities," he has nothing to say. Surely the simple-souled artist may leave such matters for the philosophers and theologians to deal with. Surely his "message" is as significant as theirs. Irving is admirable not mainly because he "wrote beautifully," but because he said something which no one else could say: he uttered the most meaning of all messages— himself. . . .

Evidently Irving . . . owed his amazing influence largely to his cheerful and wholesome this-worldliness. He was a sentimentalist, but . . . [his] tone . . . , in sentiment or in humor, is the clear and even utterance of a healthy nature.

—Henry W. Boynton, American critic, 1901
(Washington Irving)

Irving and Longfellow were primarily translators and interpreters of the Old World to the New; to them was due in large measure the liberation of the young nation from provincialism . . . by bringing the American imagination in touch with the imagination of Europe, and reknitting the deeper ties which had been, in a way, severed by forcible separation from Old World rule. . . .

But while Irving and Longfellow were translators . . . of the Old World to the New, they were also original forces in the literature of the new country. . . .

Irving gave permanent form to the Knickerbocker tradition . . . when he created Diedrich Knickerbocker and Rip Van

Winkle; and in "The Legend of Sleepy Hollow" he was not only the forerunner of the American novelist but the first American myth-maker. . . .

The real Irving . . . was a true son of the country of which New York is the capital, and his characteristic and abiding work had behind it a city, a river, and a mountain range which were not simply the stage setting of his life, but which gave color, atmosphere, tone, to his writing.

—Hamilton Wright Mabie, American critic, 1903
(Backgrounds of Literature)

Irving was broad-minded, tolerant, amiable, incapable of envy, quick to forget an affront, and always willing to think the best of humanity. His tactfulness was due in part to his large experience of life, but more to the possession of a nature that was sweet, serene, frank, and unsophisticated. . . .

A historian of American literature says: "Irving had no message." He was not indeed enslaved by a theory literary or political; neither was he passionate for some reform and convinced that his particular reform was paramount. But he who gave the world a series of writings which, in addition to being exquisite examples of literary art, are instinct with humor, brotherly kindness, and patriotism, can hardly be said not to have had a message.

Irving rendered an immense service to the biographical study of history. Columbus, Mahomet, the princes and warriors of the Holy War, are made real to us. Nor is this all. His books help to counteract that tendency of the times to make history a recondite science. . . . That man of letters is a benefactor who, like Irving, can give his audience the main facts, expressed in terms which make history more readable even than romance.

Irving perfected the short story. His genius was fecundative. Many a writer of gift and taste and at least one writer of genius, owes Irving a debt which can be acknowledged but cannot be paid. . . .

With his stories of Dutch life he conquered a new domain. That these stories remain in their first and untarnished beauty is due to Irving's rich humor and 'golden style,' and to that indescribable quality of genius by which it lifts its creations out of the local and provincial, and endows them with a charm which all can understand and enjoy.

—Leon H. Vincent, American critic, 1906
(American Literary Masters)

[When one views Washington Irving's Sunnyside, one thinks of] the "little" American literary past . . . the small uncommodious study, the limited library, the "dear" old portrait-prints of the first half of the century . . . these things, with the beauty of the site, with the sense that the man of letters of the unimproved age, the age of processes still comparatively slow, could have wanted no deeper, softer dell for mulling material over, represent the conditions that encounter now on the spot the sharp reflection of our own increase of arrangement and loss of leisure. . . .

If we envy the spinners of prose and tellers of tales to whom our American air anciently either administered or refused sustenance, this [preserving their shrines] is all . . . that we need do for them: it exhausts, or rather it forestalls, the futilities of discrimination. Strictly critical, mooning about Wolfert's Roost [Sunnyside] of a summer Sunday, I defy even the hungriest of analysts to be: his predecessors . . . profit so there, to his rueful vision, by the splendor of their possession of better conditions than his. It has taken *our* ugly era to thrust in the railroad at the foot of the slope, among the masking trees; the railroad that is part . . . of the . . . quickened pace, the heightened fever. . . .

There was no railroad, however, till long after Irving's settlement—he survived the railroad but by a few years, and my case is simply that, disengaging *his* Sunnyside from its beautiful extensions [later additions] and arriving thus at the sense of his easy elements, easy for everything but rushing about and being rushed at, the sense of his "command" of the admirable river and the admirable country, his command of all the mildness of his life, of his pleasant powers and his ample hours, of his friends and his contemporaries and his fame and

109

his honor and his temper and, above all, of his delightful fund of reminiscence and material, I seemed to hear, in the summer sounds . . . , the last faint echo of a felicity forever gone.

—Henry James, American novelist, 1907
(The American Scene)

Irving's place in literature is secure. It depends in part, no doubt, upon his pioneer position, upon the fact that he was the first of American authors to achieve wide-spread celebrity. But that fact alone would not account for his lasting fame. . . . He was, absolutely considered, one of the best writers who in his time were using the English language for literary expression.

He knew his limitations, and kept within them. He was urged to write a novel, but instinct warned him against such an attempt, and he expressed the belief that his short stories would be oftener re-read than any novel he could have written. This was probably true, for his short stories not only created that species of composition in American literature, but provided a standard of workmanship that has hardly been surpassed since. . . . "Sleepy Hollow" and "Rip Van Winkle" are stories that have . . . almost achieved the dignity of folk-lore.

—William Morton Payne, American critic, 1910
(Leading American Essayists)

At fourteen years of age I was dippy over Washington Irving . . . and used to lie under our trees by the hour and read [his writings]. I thought *The Alhambra* was a perfect creation and I still have a lingering affection for it.

—Theodore Dreiser, American novelist, 1916
(Robert H. Elias, ed. *Letters of Theodore Dreiser,* I)

The vogue of *The Sketch Book* is perhaps not what it was during its first half century. Of how many books cannot such a thing be said? But it has never ceased to amuse, and it has long stood in the decisive position of that classic in English which youthful foreigners, from Switzerland to Japan and in most of the lands that lie between, are likely to study first in learning the English language.

To have done for a hundred years what Addison with his *Spectator* did the hundred years before points to a vitality in Mr. Crayon [Washington Irving] which not a few of us may have overlooked. We have been taking him for granted, as a natural part of the landscape of letters, hardly conscious how much we should lack if he had never lived.

—Anonymous American critic, 1919
(Nation)

The native author of any genuine force and originality is almost invariably found to be under strong foreign influences, either English or Continental. It was so in the earliest days. . . . Irving, as H. R. Haweis has said, "took to England as a duck takes to water." [1920, *Prejudices, 2nd Series*]

Irving was simply a New York Englishman.
—H. L. Mencken, American critic, 1920–1924
[1924, *Prejudices, 4th Series*]

Irving's role, as man, as writer, as statesman, was to meliorate, to reconcile, to give pleasure, to refine. . . . We may suggest in passing that no other man has given a nickname to a great city, a nickname to its inhabitants, so that even to-day, as in the day of *Salmagundi,* we New Yorkers are "Gothamites" (Gotham being that English town whose wise men could be depended upon to speak nonsense) and New York is "Father Knickerbocker." . . . In concluding, we must with emphasis recur to the thought that it was Irving, more than any other man, who brought into accord the English-speaking peoples; that it was Irving who through his legends and his descriptions developed in his countrymen local sentiment and pride in the natural grandeur of their land.

—George S. Hellman, American biographer, 1925
(Washington Irving Esquire)

111

Irving's business in life was to loaf and invite the picturesque. A confirmed rambler in pleasant places, in the many lands he visited he was a lover of the past rather than the present, seeking to recreate the golden days of the Alhambra or live over the adventurous mood of the fur trader. The immediate and the actual was an unsatisfying diet for his dreams. There was in him nothing of the calm aloofness of the intellectual that stands apart to clarify its critical estimate, and none of the reforming zeal of the Puritan that is at peace only in the thick of a moral crusade. . . .

The most distinguished of our early romantics, Irving in the end was immolated on the altar of romanticism. The pursuit of the picturesque lured him away into sterile wastes, and when the will-o'-the-wisp was gone he was left empty. A born humorist . . . he was lacking in a brooding intellectuality, and instead of coming upon irony at the bottom of the cup— as the greater humorists have come upon it after life has had its way with them—he found there only sentiment and the dreamy poetic. . . .

So long as youth and high spirits endured, his inkwell was a never-failing source of gayety, but as the sparkle subsided he over-sweetened his wine. This suffices to account for the fact that all his better work was done early; and this explains why the Knickerbocker *History* remains the most genial and vital of his volumes. The gayety of youth bubbles and effervesces in those magic pages, defying time to do its worst. The critic may charge the later Irving with many and heavy shortcomings, but the romantic smoke-clouds that ascend from Wouter Van Twiller's pipe cannot be dissipated by the winds of criticism.

—Vernon Louis Parrington, American critic, 1927
(The Romantic Revolution in America 1800–1860)

A gentleman in easy circumstances, he sedulously avoided all his years any thinking on fundamental subjects; a man either timid or cool, he let all the major experiences of life escape him. He [Irving] studied, traveled and observed. This elegant writer was a strange enough product for a country and a polity supposedly new. But the Federalist gentry, no more than their

112

present descendants, shared that vision of a renewal of life in a New World which, then as now, dwelt forlornly enough in some immigrant breast. . . .

The cultivated American became the most proper of men and, from Washington Irving to Brander Matthews, feared nothing so much as any idea, gesture, sentiment or mannerism that might fundamentally differentiate him from the upper middle class of England.

—Ludwig Lewisohn, American critic, 1932
(Expression in America)

The *influence* of Irving . . . cannot for a moment be made light of. His great European fame tremendously impressed the rising generation of American writers. He set the bells to ringing and he dictated the literary forms of two decades and perhaps three. In more ways than one he was a molding force:

1. He made the shortened form of fiction popular. With "Rip Van Winkle" he became the first prominent writer of the "American short story."

2. He was a leading influence in the stripping of the moral and the didactic from the prose-tale and the periodical essay.

3. He used with effectiveness American backgrounds and American legends. His seven Knickerbocker tales—"Rip Van Winkle," "The Legend of Sleepy Hollow," "Dolph Heyliger," "The Devil and Tom Walker," "Wolfert Weber," "The Adventures of the Black Fisherman," and "Guests from Gibbet Island"—in the 1820's and 1830's had a numerous progeny.

4. He added humor to the short story, and lightness of touch. Humor it was of the eighteenth-century type, but as Irving handled it, it seemed new and attractive.

5. And finally he threw over all his work a charm of style and an atmosphere of serenity and genial beauty. To many critics this was Irving's chief contribution to American literature, and to some New Englanders at least it was his only contribution. To Emerson, Irving was "only a word-catcher." Perhaps he was, and yet it is by no means a calamity that our pioneer writer should have begun with a literary style that has been the despair of all his followers.

113

A life-work of fragments, of improvisations according to mood, task-work often thrown off for the moment, of style flowing and genial but all too often without substance. . . . May it not be that the pitiful lack of masculinity, the softness and sentimentality of our mid-century literature, came from following too closely this first great model, this first American to win European approval?

—Fred Lewis Pattee, American critic, 1935
(The First Century of American Literature)

Test *The Sketch Book,* as it stands among the sets of English classics. Test it not . . . by single essays or groups of essays . . . but as one book, the first serious writing of Washington Irving. It will then appear to be a miscellaneous and, especially, an uneven work. As literature, at least a half-dozen are worthless; twice that number bear the stigma of mediocrity. . . . [Irving's] tone is too varied, ill-sustained; reading in 1823 the *Essays of Elia,* of whose author he was somewhat contemptuous, he may have noted wherein he had failed. Lamb had written a book, but his was no book at all; it was a sheaf of Geoffrey Crayon's random drawings.

To-day the reader turns, in *The Sketch Book,* to a few essays. These are different; they live on in the speech of men, in quotation and allusion, in painting and the drama, and in innumerable reprintings. However tepid, however archaic *The Sketch Book* as a whole, these few essays seem to have life. . . .

Concerning the titles of these few there will be disagreement, but such a group might include "Rip Van Winkle," "The Boar's Head Tavern, Eastcheap," "The Mutability of Literature," "Westminster Abbey," "Stratford-on-Avon," and "The Legend of Sleepy Hollow." These still retain their hold upon the imagination, not because they are cleansed of Irving's minor sins: the commonplace metaphors, the excessive sentiment, the thinness, which bored Hazlitt. Their merits are positive. In all are Irving's long, indolent sentences, with their select vocabulary and their perfect concatenation. In all is the tranquil manner which engaged the admiration of Poe; the felicity of phrase, whose attainment may be traced in the notebooks; and the clever turn of incident, as in the conclusion of "Rip Van Winkle." . . .

In Irving's earlier writing his theme of *tempus edax rerum* [time, devourer of all things] is bluntly spoken; but in "Rip Van Winkle" we wonder a little. Here, in the dreamy story of the long slumber in the hills is implication—implication, perhaps, . . . concerning the consequences wrought by political revolution, but, more especially, concerning that relentless river of time which devours us all, whether or not we sleep, like Rip Van Winkle, for twenty years.

Mutability, indeed, the poet's strain—this is the motif of the six essays. In his five years in England this feeling overshadowed all others in Irving's mind; and in moments it found a not ignoble expression. Certainly the emotion of Rip Van Winkle, after his descent from the mountains, reflects the dejection, so unescapable in the notebooks, of the pathos of changes effected in absence. To state airily that Irving, depressed by his own isolation, was like the prodigal of the village, is to go too far. Yet symbolism is in the role; it was Irving's way of intimating his dismay in the face of this law of life.

> —Stanley T. Williams, American biographer, 1935
> *(The Life of Washington Irving, I)*

It was Irving's musical, rhythmical style, his quiet humor and dreamy charm that accounted for the triumph of the *Sketch Book* on both sides of the ocean; for, while it was published first in America, English readers were also drawn by the modesty, sweetness and candor of this American author. They were happy to see their world reflected in a mind so accomplished and winning, and they were as much surprised by the style as if a Chinese—as Irving said—had expressed himself in pure English. This style, so elegant and so simple, was to mark all of Irving's work, the sign of his cheerful good nature and transparent good taste. . . .

Fortunate Irving. . . . With his weathercock mind and uncertain talent, he had reason to bless the Sunday morning when the story of Sleepy Hollow popped into his head. He had been walking with his brother over Westminster Bridge and got to telling the old Dutch Tarrytown stories, and the notion suddenly struck him,—a book!—and he left his brother to go to church and hurried back to his lodgings and took up his pen. He jotted down some notes for the following day, and then, in the darkest of London fogs, by the light of a Monday morning candle, he wrote the tale that sped all over Europe. . . .

He . . . was destined to outlive many authors of higher power because of his tempered sweetness, geniality and grace; and, while [later] almost everyone remarked that Irving was "much overrated," still everyone continued to read him. His style, Poe said, was inimitable, and the sheer pleasantness of his mind was always to win fresh readers for Washington Irving.

—Van Wyck Brooks, American critic, 1944
(The World of Washington Irving)

Neglect of form, a vehement style, and a rude vigor of thought didn't prove to be qualities that would distinguish American authors as a group. On the contrary, most of the good ones, beginning with Washington Irving, were stylists, and a few were great stylists. [1947, *The Literary Situation*]

The colonists needed myths of their own, and, in the course of time, they created a fairly extensive native folklore. . . . More than in any other country it has been created by professional writers.

Those writers knew what they were doing, as anyone can learn for himself by studying their journals and correspondence. When they wrote to their friends about literary problems, they often used words like "legend," "mystery," "tradition," "picturesque," and "romance." All the words refer to the same quality, one that they felt was lacking in American life; Washington Irving defined it as "the color of romance and tradition." . . .

Irving, for example, set out to people the Hudson Valley with ancestral ghosts and rather jovial demons. He invented some legends of the supernatural, heard others in Dutch villages along the river, and borrowed still others from European literature, as, for example, the plot of "Rip Van Winkle," which he found in a German book and moved to the Catskills.

—Malcolm Cowley, American critic, 1944–1947
[1970, *A Many-Windowed House*]

Irving's reputation rests on his trivial work, while his more ambitious undertakings, like his five-volume life of Washington, lie heavily on the shelves. Lacking the sustaining qualities of a great imagination, his sensitive versatility made him an ideal moderator of differences between past and present, Europe and America. Because his undoubted genius fitted so exactly the role he was called upon to play, he became the first purely cultural ambassador from the New World to the Old, the first American man of letters to gain international fame.

—Robert Spiller, American critic, 1955
(The Cycle of American Literature)

He had a style, he had a temperament, he had an eye for the humors, . . . he could say . . . : While we create a new society in a new republic, let us not forget the mellowness of the age we have left behind us overseas, let us not forget the graces of life, let us not forget to be gentlemen. . . . He made Spain glamorous, England picturesque, and his own land conscious of values not to be found in industry, morals, or politics.

A slight achievement beside Wordsworth's, a modest ambition by comparison with Byron's, but enough. Not a great man, not even a great author, though a good chronicler, an excellent story-teller, a skilful essayist, an adept in romantic coloring; not in accord with progress in America but the most winning spokesman for the Federalist hope; a musician with few themes, and the minor ones the best, and many played perfectly—that is Washington Irving.

—Henry Seidel Canby, American critic, 1959
(Classic Americans)

In the field of prose fiction before the [Civil] war, the American writers, both North and South, had a verbose untidy model in the novels of Walter Scott. . . . But the narrative style of Scott, which is animated as well as copious, was rarely carried on by his imitators, whose tempo today seems intolerably slow.

We find this in Washington Irving, who combines this slow pace and this plethora [excess] of words with the meditative tone of the *Spectator*. . . . In the case of all these writers. . . . the relative lack of movement is quite in keeping with the tempo of secluded lives, of men in a position to live by themselves, usually in the country.

—Edmund Wilson, American critic, 1962
(Patriotic Gore)

Modern detractors of Irving, like modern detractors of Longfellow, have generally been distressed over the fact that he was neither Herman Melville nor Ernest Hemingway. This much is undeniable, but why it should occasion so much distress is not quite clear. That he was a "genteel" writer admits of no doubt, but in his time "genteel" was not a dirty word.

When he was seventy-five years old, he wrote a letter to a young relative not yet out of his teens, in which he described the personal qualities he admired:

I have always valued in you what I considered to be an honorable nature; a conscientiousness in regard to duties; an open truthfulness; an absence of all low propensities and sensual indulgences; a reverence for sacred things; a respect for others; a freedom from selfishness, and a prompt decision to oblige; and, with all these, a gayety of spirit, flowing, I believe, from an uncorrupted heart, that gladdens everything around you.

His own possession of all these qualities was far above the average. And he valued their manifestation of themselves in books as well as in men.

It was not his function either to scale the heights or sound the depths of life; neither did he ever pretend to be able to do so. Though he was never so indifferent to either ideas or social evils as his critics would have us believe, he consistently inhabited a middle region which he surveyed and described with a winning, companionable charm. If you must have death in the afternoon and an orgy at night, he has nothing for you. And if life is flat and meaningless to you except in moments of rare spiritual ecstacy, he has nothing for you either.

Between the heights and the depths, however, there still lies a very wide and attractive area. The reading public which dwells there may be smug, and it may be dull, but it does not need to be kicked every few minutes to stay awake, and it is possible that the tides of life run higher and stronger here than in many other publics, and that it will survive longer. This is the area that Irving inhabits, and whatever other shortcomings it may have, there can be no question that it embraces a good deal of what we generally mean to indicate when we speak of civilization.

—Edward Wagenknecht, American critic, 1962
(Washington Irving: Moderation Displayed)

We need not quarrel with Irving for not attempting what he could not and *knew* he could not do well. It is enough if we are to appreciate his doing so well with so little. His success is owing largely to his husbanding his slender store of genius and measuring out carefully his slim stock-in-trade. . . .

He believed he could do his countrymen a greater service chronicling Hudson River legends and bringing to them a touch of merry England and romantic Spain than by overtaking his talents and tiring his readers' patience with moral or philosophical disquisitions; he calculated correctly that as an intermediary between old-world culture and new-world rawness and as a romancer in the sphere of belles-lettres he would speak to better purpose than as politician or preacher.

"I have attempted no lofty theme, nor sought to look wise and learned, which appears to be very much the fashion among our American writers at present. . . . I seek only to blow a flute accompaniment in the national concert, and leave others to play the fiddle and French horn."

This careful calculation of his own potential labels him less the amateur toying with esoteric aspirations beyond his reach than the canny professional gauging his grasp by his reach.

—Henry A. Pochmann, American editor, 1967
(Essays on American Literature in Honor of
Jay B. Hubbell, Clarence Gohdes, ed.)

Epilogue

Criticism of Washington Irving falls into three fairly well-defined periods. At the beginning of the nineteenth century, he was acclaimed as the "American [who] . . . dared to rival our standard [British] writers" *(Literary Museum)* and by his success first "altered . . . the tone of our haughty [British] reviewers" *(London Magazine)*. Sir Walter Scott reported that "our sides have been absolutely sore with laughing" at *Knickerbocker's History of New York*. "Crayon [Irving's *Sketch Book*] is very good," pronounced Byron. American critics praised Irving to the skies for his humor, sentiment, and style.

Later in the century a mild reaction set in. Compared to the new generation of Poe, Hawthorne, Melville and Whitman, Irving appeared to certain anonymous critics and to Poe himself "flimsy" and "voluble"—"much overrated," a writer of "tame propriety." Ralph Waldo Emerson found him to be "imitative" and to "lack nerve and dagger." Yet his preeminence as "the first ambassador whom the New World of Letters sent to the Old" (William Makepeace Thackeray) was not seriously challenged. Although "his face was set towards the past, not towards the future" (Charles Dudley Warner), the "everliving charm of [his] style" (James Russell Lowell) was thought to make up for this; and he was accepted as a literary monument long before his death.

Finally, twentieth-century critics have attempted a closer examination of Irving's work and have sought the man behind the monument. They have revealed emotional and financial crises in his supposedly serene life and have noted "anti-Establishment" positions in his writings—for example, his satire on money getting and his defense of the Indians. They have spotlighted his sophisticated appreciation of "the graces of [European] life" (Henry Seidel Canby). While some have emphasized the limitations of Washington Irving —"this elegant writer . . . [who] let all the major experiences of life escape him" (Ludwig Lewisohn)—others have defended his concentration on life's "middle region which he surveyed and described with a winning, companionable charm" (Edward Wagenknecht).

Basically noncontroversial, Washington Irving remains as readable today, in his best work, as he was a century and a half ago. Later authors who aimed at greater originality or profounder ideas may not be read as long as this hardworking professional. Even an unsympathetic critic, Vernon Parrington, succumbs to the spell of Irving's writings and confesses: "The romantic smoke-clouds that ascend from Wouter Van Twiller's pipe cannot be dissipated by the winds of criticism."

THE WORKS OF
WASHINGTON IRVING

1802–1803	*Letters of Jonathan Oldstyle, Gent.*
1807–1808	*Salmagundi*
1809	*Knickerbocker's History of New York*
1819–1820	*The Sketch Book*
1822	*Bracebridge Hall*
1824	*Tales of a Traveller*
1828	*The Life of Voyages of Christopher Columbus*
1829	*The Conquest of Granada*
1831	*Voyages and Discoveries of the Companions of Columbus*
1832	*The Alhambra*
1835	*The Crayon Miscellany* (including *A Tour on the Prairies*)
1836	*Astoria*
1837	*The Adventures of Captain Bonneville, U.S.A.*
1840	*The Life of Oliver Goldsmith, with Selections from His Writings*
1841	*Biography and Poetical Remains of the Late Margaret Miller Davidson*
1849	*The Life of Oliver Goldsmith* (revised, enlarged edition)
1850	*Mahomet and His Successors*
1855	*Wolfert's Roost*
1855–1859	*Life of George Washington*

SELECTED BIBLIOGRAPHY

WASHINGTON IRVING'S WRITINGS

Works. New York, G. P. Putnam's Sons, 1850–1888. 10 vols.

Representative Selections, Henry A. Pochmann, ed. New York, American Book Company, 1934.

Journals, William P. Trent and George S. Hellman, ed. Boston, The Bibliophile Society, 1919. 3 vols.

BOOKS ABOUT WASHINGTON IRVING

BOWERS, CLAUDE G., *The Spanish Adventures of Washington Irving.* Boston, Houghton Mifflin Company, 1940.

HELLMAN, GEORGE SIDNEY, *Washington Irving, Esquire: Ambassador at Large from the New World to the Old.* New York, Alfred A. Knopf, 1925.

IRVING, PIERRE M., *The Life and Letters of Washington Irving.* New York, G. P. Putnam, 1862–1864. 4 vols.

LANGFIELD, WILLIAM R., *Washington Irving: A Bibliography.* New York, New York Public Library, 1933.

REICHART, WALTER A., *Washington Irving and Germany.* Ann Arbor, University of Michigan Press, 1957.

WAGENKNECHT, EDWARD, *Washington Irving: Moderation Displayed.* New York, Oxford University Press, 1962.

WILLIAMS, STANLEY T., *The Life of Washington Irving.* New York, Oxford University Press, 1935. 2 vols.

Index

ABOUT THE AUTHOR

George Sanderlin has become well known for his books which combine historical source material with a lively narrative.

Examples of his masterful work in this genre are *Ben Franklin: As Others Saw Him* and *The Settlement of California,* both published by Coward, McCann & Geoghegan. His books have been widely praised for their success in giving the immediacy of the present to events of the past.

A professor of English at San Diego State College, Mr. Sanderlin received the California State University and Colleges Award for an Outstanding Professor for 1973-74. He and his wife live near El Cajon, California.

DATE DUE